# CHEMICAL AND BIOLOGICAL WARFARE

Also by Elaine Landau

WEIGHT:
A Teenage Concern

# CHEMICAL AND BIOLOGICAL WARFARE

Elaine Landau

Lodestar Books
DUTTON    NEW YORK

Copyright © 1991 by Elaine Landau

All rights reserved. No part of this publication may be reproduced or transmitted in any form or by any means, electronic or mechanical, including photocopy, recording, or any information storage or retrieval system now known or to be invented, without permission in writing from the publisher, except by a reviewer who wishes to quote brief passages in connection with a review written for inclusion in a magazine, newspaper, or broadcast.

*Library of Congress Cataloging-in-Publication Data*

Landau, Elaine.
   Chemical and biological warfare / Elaine Landau.—1st ed.
     p. cm.
   Includes bibliographical references (p.    ) and index.
   Summary: Discusses chemical and biological weapons, from tear and nerve gases to anthrax and rice blast, examining the effects, political significance, deterrents, and moral and ethical issues.
   ISBN 0-525-67364-4
   1. Chemical warfare—Juvenile literature.  2. Biological warfare—Juvenile literature.  [1. Chemical warfare. 2. Biological warfare.]  I. Title.
UG447.L25   1991
358'.3—dc20                                                           91-15416
                                                                                  CIP
                                                                                    AC

Published in the United States by Lodestar Books, an affiliate of Dutton Children's Books, a division of Penguin Books USA Inc., 375 Hudson Street, New York, N.Y. 10014

Published simultaneously in Canada by McClelland & Stewart, Toronto

Editor: Virginia Buckley    Designer: Richard Granald, LMD
Printed in the U.S.A.    First Edition    10 9 8 7 6 5 4 3 2

for the wonderful telephone reference librarians at the Morris County Library in New Jersey, who so expertly provide information

# CONTENTS

| | | |
|---|---|---|
| 1 | An Invisible Weapon | 1 |
| 2 | A Killing Catalog: Chemical Weapons | 28 |
| 3 | A Killing Catalog: Biological Weapons | 42 |
| 4 | Early Developments | 51 |
| 5 | "Trust but Verify" | 67 |
| 6 | Danger! Environmental and Moral Risks | 82 |
| | Organizations Concerned with Peace and Disarmament | 103 |
| | End Notes | 107 |
| | Further Readings | 111 |
| | Index | 115 |

# 1
# AN INVISIBLE WEAPON

Without warning, an invisible killer, delivered by a missile warhead, silently descends through the air on an unsuspecting population. Initially, only a foul, garlic-like odor comes from the yellowish haze that settles on the town. Yet before long, the effects on its victims are all too apparent. First they experience blurred vision, sneezing and coughing fits, and nausea, followed by excessive vomiting. Once the spreading inflammation invades the respiratory tract, breathing becomes difficult, and large, painful, ulcerated blisters soon erupt in their groins and armpits.

Some suffer slow, excruciating deaths. Others survive, only to learn later that their bone marrow has been affected, limiting their body's ability to manufacture the white cells needed to fight infection. All of these individuals are the unfortunate victims of chemical weapons—once dubbed "the hellish poison."

This nightmarish tool of war was unleashed by the Iraqi military during its eight-year conflict (1980–1988) with Iran in the Persian Gulf. In doing so, Iraq violated the Geneva Protocol of 1925, an international agreement signed by 129 nations (including Iraq), which prohibits the use of chemical weapons. Yet, despite initial denials from Iraqi sources, there was little doubt that such weapons had been used. United Nations field investigations were requested by Iran in March 1984, April 1985, and February 1986. Relying on the judgment of four impartial chemical-weapons experts, these investigations yielded the following conclusions:

"There had been repeated use of chemical weapons against Iranian forces by Iraqi forces, employing aerial bombs and very probably rockets. The chemical agents used were mustard gas (yperite) and probably, on some occasions, nerve agents. "A new dimension of the situation was that civilians in Iran also had been injured by chemical weapons."[1]

In March and August of 1988, Iran again asked United Nations observers to investigate Iraqi atrocities. This time Iraq had unleashed poison gas on the Kurdish town of Halabja. Ironically, Halabja is a town in northern Iraq, but it was the site of some local rebellion, and only a week prior to the gas attack, Iranian troops had marched into the area.

Iraqi Defense Minister Adan Khairallah rejected Iran's request for another United Nations investigation on the grounds that it was an affront to Iraq's sovereignty. Instead, he invited an international team of journalists to survey the area. Some viewed this move as an artful ploy, since it was generally agreed that conditions apparent to the eyes of a trained observer might not be as readily perceived by a reporter.

Once the journalists assembled in Baghdad, Defense Minister Khairallah's welcome to them was followed by the caustic remark, "I was struck by the fact that you haven't brought your gas masks with you." He went on to claim that the military use of poison gas in Kurdish villages was "technically impossible." Yet, after intensive questioning by the correspondents, Khairallah admitted that he was unable to categorically deny the use of chemical weapons in the region noted. Nevertheless, he stressed that whatever occurred within Iraq's borders was an internal matter and therefore not a cause for international concern.

However, it became increasingly difficult for the Iraqi government to deny the tragedy experienced by the Kurds. Within a short period of time, the death toll mounted to over five thousand people. The streets and roads of Halabja were littered with the bloated corpses of gas victims. An additional seven thousand unarmed civilians, many of them women and children, survived but soon suffered the lingering effects of the poison gas.

Sonia Mahmoud, a local Kurdish woman, described the scene to an interpreter:

"When they dropped the chemical bomb, there was a whitish smoke. And we could see the birds fall out of the sky. And the cows in the village dropped to the ground from the effect.

"My brother was killed. But when the women leapt to their brothers' bodies, they died instantly. So nobody went there, even to go to the bodies."[2]

The Iraqis' use of chemical weapons on the Kurds was subsequently confirmed by a group of American doctors with the organization Physicians for Human Rights. These doctors treated survivors of the Halabja gas attack who fled to refugee camps in nearby Turkey. Although the physicians weren't positive, they generally agreed that the effects they observed were caused by mustard gas laced with hydrogen cyanide.

In evaluating the Gulf situation, United Nations experts emphasized the special horror of using poison gas. They stated that chemical weapons are "inhumane [and] indiscriminate in their action and cause long-term disabilities and suffering." They also felt that ongoing use of chemical weapons in the Iraq–Iran war set the stage for reliance on these arms in any future conflicts.

United Nations Secretary Javier Pérez de Cuellar stressed that Iraq's violation of the Protocol ban on chemical weapons constituted "one of the gravest infringements of international norms." He unequivocally urged the world's nations to exert concerted political pressure to insure that the agreement be upheld. President-elect George Bush expressed his revulsion over the gas attacks in the fall of 1988, after reviewing photographs of Kurdish civilians who had been gassed to death. He said, "I thought we had relegated the horrors of chemical warfare to the history books. I thought we had banished forever what we all saw only a few months ago—a mother trying to protect her child, waving her arms against the invisible winds of death."[3]

Yet, despite moving rhetoric from a number of factions, Iraq persisted in its use of chemical weapons for many years without any significant international censure. Perhaps this was possible because some nations had less than noble motives. It has been suggested that, because the United States and France considered Iran a mutual foe, they did not initially express moral outrage at Iraq's use of chemical weapons.

As Peter Galbraith of the Senate Foreign Relations Committee staff put it: "I think it's fair to say that the Iraqis used chemical weapons against the Kurdish civilians precisely because they'd gotten away with it, using it against the Iranians.

"Among other things, we reestablished diplomatic

relations in November 1984, after their first use of chemical weapons. So they had good reason to believe that they could get away with murder, and that's just what they did."[4]

Other factors influenced the conspicuous silence as well. While some French officials verbally deplored the use of chemical weapons by any nation, others were mindful of a debt that Baghdad still owed Paris for other weapons purchased during the continuing hostilities between Iraq and Iran. These officials feared that interference would result in nonpayment of several million dollars.

In addition, because France, Britain, Italy, and Germany were vying for potentially lucrative contracts to rebuild Iraq after the war, none were anxious to alienate the rising Third World power. The British were especially cautious in their criticism of Iraq, lest they appear to be currying favor with Iran as a means of securing the release of British hostages held by pro-Iranian terrorist groups in Lebanon.

Arab nations were also reluctant to speak out against Iraq and its leader, Saddam Hussein. During the conflict, Egypt, Saudi Arabia, and Jordan favored Iraq's government over Iran's regime. Besides, none of these Arab nations wanted to antagonize Iraq, which had the greatest military might in the region, as well as the fourth largest army in the world.

In recent years, Iraq and a number of other Third World countries began building chemical-weapons arsenals. Manufacturing these lethal armaments is not a complex process; any nation with a pesticide factory is already equipped to do so. As a former deputy chief of staff for France's air force said, "Chemical weapons are the poor man's weapon. They are cheap, simple to use—and very, very effective." These sentiments were echoed by Graham Pearson, a leading figure in Britain's defensive chemical-warfare program, when he said, "It's a relatively low-tech operation, and Third World countries appear to be able to obtain aircraft and bombs that they can easily modify to deliver chemical weapons."

United States intelligence sources report that twenty to thirty countries are currently capable of manufacturing chemical weapons. Even worse, a number of Third World nations are also acquiring long-range ballistic missiles, which would enable them to strike targets hundreds of miles away with an array of poison gases.

How did these Third World countries amass this impressive assortment of deadly chemicals and hardware? The ease of access was directly related to the overabundance of weapons accumulated by larger powers in past decades. This proliferation resulted in a wide range of stockpiled artillery and rockets, which were eventually made available for sale. As Third World countries became the eager consumers of these superfluous commodities, a few Middle Eastern nations built up a substantial quantity of armaments.

Hardware could be purchased openly, but the Geneva Protocol of 1925 made it necessary to rely on subterfuge to secure the chemicals to create the desired weaponry. In 1983 Iraq purchased a chemical known as thiodiglycol from the Phillips Petroleum Company in Oklahoma. Alone, the chemical, which is frequently used in ball-point-pen ink, is harmless. But when it is mixed with hydrochloric acid, the deadly chemical weapon mustard gas is produced.

The Iraqis also bought five hundred tons of hydrochloric acid from a Dutch concern. The Dutch manufacturers were told that the substance was to be shipped to a pesticide factory in Samarra, Iraq. After receiving a second substantial order for the chemical, plant officials began to suspect that perhaps these massive quantities were not intended to be used to rid the nation of harmful insect pests.

However, there is little doubt internationally that Germany has been the worst culprit in supplying Third World countries with the means to produce chemical-weapons arsenals. Despite early denials by the German government, a number of German chemical companies knowingly engaged in such sales. As a British chemical expert bitterly described the situation, "German businessmen have no scruples. They supplied nuclear technology to Pakistan. Then they exported products intended to gas Iranian soldiers, who sometimes go for treatment to hospitals near Frankfurt."

German chemical companies were also held largely responsible for assisting Libyan leader Muammar Qaddafi in constructing the Third World's largest chemical-weapons facility. Qaddafi's Libyan plant was believed to have the capacity to produce forty tons of both nerve gas and mustard gas monthly.

Prior to its completion, U.S. intelligence sources learned that Qaddafi's massive chemical-weapons facility was located in Rabata, a deserted area about forty miles southwest of Tripoli. Although Qaddafi asserted that the factory was to be a pharmaceutical plant and would not be used to manufacture lethal chemical weapons, few believed him. Instead, the dictator's political sympathies and his general acceptance of terrorism as a legitimate alternative provoked concern among many nations as to his real intentions.

Qaddafi's credibility was further called into question by the plant's physical structure. The walls and floors were paneled with acid-resistant tile; sensors to detect escaping gas, as well as companion alarm devices, stood mounted throughout the building. A thick outer wall circled the entire plant, and the facility was monitored twenty-four hours a day with video cameras. Even during the earliest stages of its construction, only authorized personnel were permitted on the site. The radar devices and antiaircraft missiles near the premises also seemed inappropriate for an innocuous pharmaceutical plant.

When U.S. officials initially charged that German chemical concerns were instrumental in Qaddafi's plans, the German government firmly disavowed such involvement. Although German politicians were outraged by the United States' continuing allegations, U.S. intelligence secured irrefutable data, such as satellite photos, plant blueprints, and documented on-site observations, to support their claims. Thus confronted, the German government was forced to reopen its hastily closed investigation of chemical plants that were dealing with Third World powers. A tip from the United States led them to documents implicating over thirty German companies, as well as some from other nations.

Shortly thereafter, a German weekly magazine charged that the German chemical company Imhausen-Chemie had assembled "everything that is needed to build a chemical plant." Details regarding these materials were sent to a Frankfurt firm known as IBI, which stands for Ihsan Barbouti International. Ihsan Barbouti is an Iraqi businessman who, Western intelligence sources believe, acted as the key broker for Qaddafi's chemical factory.

After negotiating for the necessary chemical components from Imhausen-Chemie, Barbouti arranged, through his newly opened Hong Kong office, to have the chemicals sent to Imhausen's Hong Kong branch. From there the materials were shipped to Libya on a Belgian freighter. It was hoped that this circuitous route would divert attention from the questionable cargo. However, once the ploy was discovered, the Belgian government charged the ship's owner with falsifying the shipping documents for the transaction.

Although Barbouti admits designing the Rabata complex, as well as purchasing its materials and supplies, he insists that the facility was to be used only to manufacture medications. Yet many countries doubt Barbouti's innocence. This may be because his company had already secured the protective clothing and equipment used in handling chemical weapons for the workers in the Rabata facility.

During the four years Ihsan Barbouti was employed by Libya, he established and maintained a network of businesses that spanned numerous countries, from Europe to Asia. Barbouti was especially drawn to Germany because their export licensing rules are exceedingly lenient. Barbouti amassed a personal fortune of over one hundred million dollars by dealing in illicit chemical weapons. However, both the Iraqi and German governments have launched criminal investigations regarding Barbouti's role in helping Libya to secure chemical weapons, and English and Scottish tax courts are examining his business transactions in their countries.

After public exposure of its negligence, the German government finally initiated legal action against firms suspected of chemical-weapons dealings with Libya.

Having admitted to taking an active role in the Rabata plant's development while heading the Imhausen-Chemie Company, Hippenstiel Imhausen was found guilty of selling chemical weapons. While on the witness stand in a German court of law, Imhausen stated that, soon after securing the one-hundred-and-fifty-million-dollar contract from Qaddafi, he realized that the proposed facility would be used to manufacture nerve gas rather than pharmaceuticals and pesticides. Nevertheless, he established a bogus branch of his company in Hong Kong to camouflage the project's actual intent. As a result of these dealings, the German businessman realized over twelve million dollars in personal profits.

Yet, despite Imhausen's conviction, it is difficult to be optimistic about comparable pending court cases. Frequently German law so favors private business that it is nearly impossible for government agencies to detect and correct wrongdoings. In a number of cases, "not guilty" verdicts have been given to repeat offenders, who then continue to conduct questionable international transactions.

Ironically, one of the few organizations in Germany to be punished for its part in a chemical-weapons export scandal was a public-interest group known as the Society for Threatened Peoples. In 1984 the organization openly accused a German chemical company of contributing to political mass murder by supplying Iraq with chemical-weapons materials.

The company responded by suing the Society for Threatened Peoples for libel. Perhaps the firm won the case because the group had based its claims on articles in the American press, which the court claimed weren't sufficient evidence. A German customs officer may have best summarized the situation when he said, "I think there's a lot more political commitment in the United States to enforce these laws than there is in Germany."[5] Unfortunately, he may be exactly on target in his assessment. A U.S. State Department official recently noted that German chemical concerns "assisted Iran, Iraq, and Syria in acquiring chemical-weapons capability" and that "there is still evidence of ongoing contacts between German companies and these countries."[6]

Equally disturbing is Japan's role in helping Libya secure chemical weapons. U.S. intelligence sources learned that a company called Japan Steel Works was instrumental in constructing a metal-works facility close to the Rabata chemical plant. The firm also sent staff to Libya to produce bomb castings for chemical weapons.

As early as 1988, American officials questioned Tokyo regarding the possible involvement of Japanese companies in Qaddafi's chemical plant, but the Japanese were evasive. Later, when the United States alleged that Japan Steel Works employees were still assisting at Libya's chemical plant, a diplomat from Japan's U.S. embassy explained that this was a case of mistaken identity. He told American officials that Japan Steel Works employees had neglected to take their uniforms when they left Libya. The new Asian workers were, the Japanese official suggested, possibly Thai, but his explanation was considered highly unlikely.

Intelligence sources reported that successful chemical test runs were performed at Libya's soon-to-be-completed plant. But, just when it seemed as if the facility was ready to begin operating, things began to go amiss. After U.S. protests fully revealed Qaddafi's true purpose to the world community, it became increasingly difficult for the Libyan leader to obtain the final materials he needed. But that was a minor obstacle compared to the extensive damage done to the plant when fire swept through it in March 1990. Some reports even stated that the facility had burned to the ground. U.S. sources later revealed that, although the fire managed to "incinerate the main production block," the huge holding tanks storing the weapon components were unharmed.

While the international community wondered how the blaze had begun, White House spokesperson Marlin Fitzwater refuted insinuations that the United States had engaged in arson in this instance. He said, "We deny we had any involvement. We just dare not speculate on the cause."[7]

Diplomatic sources around the world debated over whether the fire was the result of an accident, sabotage, or an attack. There were some indications that the blaze might have begun by chance. Once international pressure began to mount, a substantial number of skilled foreign chemists quickly vacated the area. Since the production of chemical weapons involves the use of highly flammable substances, some thought the inexperienced, poorly trained Libyan technicians left at the site might have made a critical error.

But Libya pointed the finger of blame at three possible sources—the United States, Israel, and, surprisingly, Germany. Although construction of the facility was largely made possible through the expertise and assistance of German firms, there was speculation that the German government might now wish to rectify this embarrassing fact. While Germany did not acknowledge Libya's accusation, Israel simply echoed the U.S.

denial, stating that it knew nothing about the incident's origin.

Even though for a time it looked as if the Libyan chemical-weapons threat might be curtailed, evidence to the contrary soon surfaced. U.S. intelligence sources learned that Qaddafi might be constructing a new underground chemical-weapons plant at a remote location hundreds of miles from Tripoli. Some also think that the Rabata fire was merely a ploy to divert attention from Libya's more intensive efforts to produce chemical weapons at the undisclosed underground plant. Two German chemical companies, as well as a Dutch firm, were believed to be supplying Libya with components to manufacture chemical weapons at the secret facility.

However, predictions about Libya's chemical-weapons capacity again shifted when U.S. officials learned that the original Rabata plant had been restored and was actively engaged in the "large-scale production" of poison gas weapons. The United States also suspects Qaddafi of digging a bunker near the Rabata plant to shield his chemicals and bomb components from aerial attacks. The German television channel ZDF reported that German companies were helping Libya to construct the underground bunker by providing both the sophisticated measuring instruments and laser technology necessary for the task. It is possible that the Libyan leader hopes to eventually maintain chemical-weapons facilities at various locations.

While Libya strove to develop chemical weapons to enhance its position as a Third World power, Iraq's Saddam Hussein relied on his substantial stash of chemical armaments to intimidate other nations that might object to his aggressive moves in the Middle East. In a region often teetering on the brink of war, the horror of such a clash was intensified by the reality that deadly chemical agents were likely to be unleashed not only on troops but on defenseless civilian populations as well.

As early as 1981, Israel, a longtime foe of Iraq, bombed Iraq's Osirak nuclear reactor, claiming that the plant was developing a nuclear bomb. More recently, Hussein threatened to use chemical weaponry on Israel if another attack on his weapons installations should occur. He said, "If Israel dares to hit even one piece of steel on any industrial site, we will make the fire eat half of Israel. . . . We don't need an atomic bomb because we have the double chemical."[8]

In citing the "double chemical," Hussein made a clear reference to binary chemical warheads, or nerve gas. Binary weapons, which usually take the form of artillery shells or missile warheads, are composed of two relatively safe compounds which, when mixed, combine to form deadly nerve gas.

Israel's position in the Middle East was further threatened after Saddam Hussein invaded Kuwait on August 2, 1990, and the possibility of a subsequent chemical-weapons attack on Israel loomed large. Although Israel has had to defend its borders on past occasions, this would have been the only war in which the first casualties were likely to be civilians.

In preparation for the worst scenario, Israeli civil defense officials issued instructions on the best protection against a chemical strike. After a television demonstration by a former Israeli civil defense officer showing how a cloth soaked in water and baking soda could suffice as a makeshift gas mask, supermarket sales of baking soda skyrocketed.

To further insure their safety, thousands of Israelis also purchased gas masks and anti-chemical suits in the month following Hussein's invasion of Kuwait. One man who bought a $140 gas mask for his young son said, "My thirteen-year-old son can't sleep at night, he's so frightened. So I'm buying him a gas mask—sort of a bar mitzvah [coming-of-age ceremony] present."

A Holocaust survivor purchased gas masks and anti-chemical suits for his entire family—including his grown children and their offspring. He explained to the store owner that he had escaped the Nazi gas chambers and didn't want to die with his family in a gas attack now. In a nation in which a sizeable portion of the population experienced Hitler's Holocaust, Hussein's gas-attack threats seemed frighteningly real. Shabtai Taibor is an Israeli citizen whose grandparents perished in Nazi gas chambers. Like thousands of others who share his heritage, Taibor knows that German firms sold Iraq the chemicals and technology to create poison gas. "The gas was zyklon-B in 1941," Taibor said. "Today it's nerve gas. But it's German gas just the same. . . . I can no longer keep the pain inside me. The Germany we thought was gone still exists."

To insure that their offspring do not experience the horrors known to past generations, some Israelis spent over two thousand dollars for special motor-driven masks for children too small to wear the standard size. There were also some inquiries about anti-chemical animal shelters for household pets. In addition to individual purchases, the Israeli government secured over 4.2 million gas masks for civilian use, which were stored in various locations throughout the nation. Following Iraq's invasion of Kuwait, these were distributed as well.

Other precautionary measures against the effects of chemical warfare have been under way in Israel for over a decade. To preserve the nation's superior air strength, the government allots 5 to 10 percent of its annual budget for airstrip protection. Conscious of the fact that a chemical-weapons strike on their airfields could disable Israeli pilots and support staff, Israelis have moved their air force to an underground location. There the nation's fighter crafts are housed and maintained in special protective hangars. The entire area is designed to resist a chemical-weapons attack, and all staff are equipped with decontamination gear.

The Israeli government also trained the nation's youth in survival strategies to combat a chemical-weapons strike. On the first day of school following Hussein's summer invasion of Kuwait, first graders did not learn the alphabet as planned. Instead, the children were instructed and drilled on what to do in the event of a chemical-weapons attack.

Israel was not the only country that invested in tangible protective measures against chemical weaponry. Saddam Hussein's invasion of Kuwait brought U.S. troops to the Middle East as part of a multinational force. American soldiers remained posted in nearby Saudi Arabia to protect U.S. interests in the region and prevent further expansionist aggression by Hussein. During their early days in the area, they learned through U.S. satellite intelligence that Iraqi troops near the border were engaged in continuous chemical-weaponry drills. If Hussein used chemical weapons in a cross-border attack on Saudi Arabia, American soldiers would be among those affected by the deadly poison.

In readiness, American troops were both trained to

# An Invisible Weapon ❑ 17

respond effectively and supplied with protective gear in which to do so. The protective "uniform" issued to soldiers facing chemical-weaponry threats looks something like an astronaut's suit. The soldier's face is covered by a tightly sealed M40 or M43 gas mask, outfitted with a communications microphone and a headphone set. His body is encased in a double-layered suit made of a synthetic gas-absorbing fabric. A gas-resistant shroud is placed over his head and shoulders, and he also has a protective helmet and rubber gloves. Besides wearing this cumbersome uniform, a soldier must carry his weapon, ammunition, a water canteen, six syringes of drugs to counteract nerve agents, towelettes soaked in a chemical that neutralizes mustard gas, and whatever other field equipment is assigned him.

Tests conducted at the army's Aberdeen Proving Ground in Maryland demonstrated how a soldier using the protective garb and equipment would soon overheat when either walking or running. This factor is especially critical if he's expected to fight an enemy in desert temperatures that reach 120 degrees Fahrenheit. Since, under the circumstances, frequent rest periods in air-conditioned environments are not feasible, the army relied on its M20 Collective Protection Equipment, which consists largely of a gas-proof plastic liner, designed for a room or tent, through which uncontaminated cool air is pumped to those within. Army tanks and other armored military vehicles were also equipped with special air-filtering systems.

Yet, despite these extra measures to keep soldiers cool and comfortable, there are undeniable disadvantages in having to contend with a possible chemical-weapons strike in extreme desert heat. Even under the best of circumstances, a soldier's weighty protective gear adds a minimum of ten degrees to the already scorching daytime temperatures, thereby increasing the possibility of dehydration and heat exhaustion. If these conditions prevail, troop efficiency could significantly drop within a matter of hours.

American soldiers are taught to combat chemical weaponry at Fort McClellan in Alabama. Since the training school began in 1987, nearly twelve thousand soldiers have completed the program. However, it may still be difficult to prepare for some aspects of chemical warfare. As Thomas L. McNaugher, Senior Fellow at the Brookings Institute, explained the predicament, "We've got to expect a certain shock if and when these things are first used in combat, just as there's going to be a shock when most of these soldiers enter combat. Most of them have never seen it. They may have to move out of position to get away from a particularly noxious gas cloud, and it kills those who are not quick enough to mask and get their suits on."[9]

A swift response is essential to surviving a chemical-weapons attack, which might occur at any hour of the day or night. According to U.S. Army Captain Terry Cloonan, "An individual soldier on the battlefield has fifteen seconds to don his protective mask. And that would include nine seconds to don it, seal it, clear it and give six additional seconds to pull the hood on, secure the zipper, and give the gas-attack signal."[10]

The multinational force of allied troops stationed in the Gulf were routinely given pyridostignine tablets. This drug enhances the effectiveness of the nerve gas antidotes they might later need in combat. Each soldier carried six syringes of nerve gas antidotes with him at all times. He was taught that the early effects of a nerve gas attack include uncontrollable drooling, mucus pouring from the nose, stomach cramps, severe headache, and blurred vision. As soon as the GI recognized these symptoms, he was to give himself the six injections. If there was a delay, the soldier would drop to the ground, experiencing severe pain and convulsions. At that point, he could no longer use the medication on his own. If a nearby soldier didn't immediately administer the shots to him, his survival was unlikely.

To cope with the worst possible consequences, army field hospital personnel were specially trained to handle casualties resulting from a chemical-weapons strike. Gas victims must be isolated from other patients and washed down with high-pressure sprays and cleaning agents such as bleach. It is essential that affected soldiers be thoroughly decontaminated before having their conventional wounds treated.

In addition to these damage-control tactics, allied forces in the Gulf also relied on preventive measures. To this end, the army used the Fox M93—a fast-moving chemical-detection vehicle. Speedy tanklike machines, they comb high-risk regions while two small wheels pick up soil samples. A vacuum hose, fondly referred to as "the sniffer," extends from the vehicle's rear to capture air samples.

Operated by a driver and two technicians, the Foxes contain an internal computer that sounds an alarm when contaminated soil or air is collected. Then large yellow fluorescent markers are left out for approaching troops to see. Vehicle operators also use the Fox's communication system to contact field commanders so that soldiers can be directed away from contaminated areas.

Although Fox crew members venture into some of the most potentially hazardous battle zones, they are safer and more comfortable than most soldiers. To insure the equipment's proper functioning, temperatures inside a Fox M93 are kept cool. The air pressure within these roving units is also sufficiently high to keep out chemical contaminants. Fox M93 drivers and technicians don't need to wear gas masks or heavy protective gear.

In still another effort to protect allied troops, large numbers of chickens were transported to the Gulf. Since fowl react to gas before humans do, it was hoped that the farm birds would provide the soldiers with an early warning of chemical attack.

Although the United States has a substantial chemical-weapons arsenal, these agents would not be used in a war against Iraq. Most political analysts feel that if a superpower even threatened to unleash poison gas or nuclear weapons on a small Third World nation, considerable international outrage would result. As one Western diplomat described the predicament, "We might gain a military chip, but lose the political war." The United States' use of chemical agents could also negatively affect future efforts to have these weapons permanently removed from the planet.

Regardless of assured reprisal from the United States, numerous military strategists speculated that Saddam Hussein might still be tempted to use chemical weapons on American soldiers if a war broke out. If U.S. troops were seriously hindered at the start, Hussein might hope that the American public would strongly protest their country's continued involvement.

There was also the possibility that Hussein would unleash deadly chemical agents to cripple or disrupt military posts, communication centers, ports, and heavily populated areas. If at any time in the conflict, the Iraqi president felt he had no chance of winning, it was believed he might drop poison-gas bombs over as much of the Middle East's oil-producing territory as possible. Such a move would be likely to create financial havoc within Western economies until the facilities could be restored to working order. As a source close to French president François Mitterand said, "The problem for the West is no longer the Soviet threat; it is the Third World."

Hostilities broke out when Saddam Hussein failed to meet the allies' January 15, 1991, deadline for his troops to withdraw from Kuwait. The multinational force conducted an intensive air-bombing campaign prior to initiating its ground offensive. The extensive air activity demolished Hussein's chemical-weapons plants. Yet, despite allied efforts to totally destroy Iraq's chemical-arms capacity, a portion of the nation's chemical arsenal survived the air bombardment. U.S. intelligence sources were uncertain how much remained, since pilots had no way of knowing if the special ammunitions bunkers they leveled were stocked with chemical or conventional weapons.

It was also believed that tons of chemical agents inside bombs, artillery shells, rockets, and short-range missiles were previously placed in strategic locations by Iraqi troops. A senior U.S. Army official told the American public to be prepared for some unsettling film footage if the Iraqis resorted to chemical warfare. He warned, "It's going to be chaos, and we're going to have a lot of casualties."

Once the allied troops began the ground war, some front-line soldiers remained in their protective chemical suits for several days. Despite their discomfort while advancing in the desert heat, they were prepared for the worst. But, as it turned out, the Iraqis did not use chemical weapons in fighting the allies.

A number of Iraqi soldiers taken prisoner reported that, although they had been ordered to fire chemical rockets at the opposition, they had refused to do so. Some were afraid of being tried as war criminals following the conflict. Others claimed that the allied ground forces had advanced too rapidly for them to launch the weapons before escaping. American military leaders suggested that the massive bombing of Iraq's launching artillery may have also been instrumental in forestalling the use of chemical weapons.

Possibly, Saddam Hussein's fear of retaliation was a factor. As one military expert analyzed the turn of events, "Saddam is completely unscrupulous, but he's not crazy." The Iraqi president may have felt confident of victory when he deployed chemical agents against Iran and the Kurds. But using them against an adversary equipped with weapons capable of even greater mass destruction was another matter. According to Marvin Feuerwerger, a strategic analyst at Johns Hopkins University, "The threat of escalation dominance may have simply deterred Saddam, who always hoped to survive the war and retain power even if defeated. He didn't know what we might do if he used gas."[11]

Throughout the hostilities, Iraq fired SCUD missiles at Israel, unsuccessfully attempting to draw the nation into the conflict.

The Israelis didn't know whether these weapons had conventional or chemical warheads, but as it turned out, chemical weapons were not deployed against the small nation. Some military experts believe Saddam did not want to chance accidentally gassing Palestinians in the area, who were among his most faithful supporters. Yet, unfortunately, the panic generated by the possible use of these weapons caused some deaths. In one air strike, three elderly women who failed to open their gas masks' air filters died of suffocation, as did the three-year-old who resisted her parents' efforts to put on her mask. A significant number of people also became ill after needlessly injecting themselves with an anti-chemical drug.

In the war's aftermath, various factions revolted against Saddam Hussein. Hussein's troops responded by attempting to squelch what was rapidly turning into a nationwide rebellion. President George Bush warned the Iraqi leader that, if chemical weapons were used on the rebels, U.S. forces would retaliate.

While Hussein did not technically resort to chemical weapons, his soldiers massacred thousands of people in napalm attacks that left the burned bodies of men, women, and children strewn along a highway in southern Iraq. There were also reports of rebel areas hit with short-range FROG-7 missiles filled with white phosphorus. This substance, generally used to mark military positions, causes severe skin burns. Iraqi helicopters dropped tear gas on rebel strongholds as well.

The future threat of chemical-weapons use in Middle East conflicts cannot be underestimated. Unfortunately, chemical attacks by foreign planes and missiles are only a portion of the problem. If chemical weaponry were ever to gain even marginal respectability, the potential for its abuse is vast.

Such unsavory means might be employed by unscrupulous dictators to eliminate pockets of rebellion within their own borders. It is known that, in addition to gassing Iraq's Kurdish population during the Iraq–Iran war, Saddam Hussein had also used chemical weapons to annihilate his own army's military deserters. Throughout that conflict, hundreds of Iraqi soldiers fled from their battalions to hide in southern Iraq's swampy terrain near the head of the Persian Gulf. Although Hussein sent in troops to bring back the deserters, most relied on the area's natural camouflage to elude capture. Annoyed by his military's inability to round up these soldiers, Hussein resolved the problem with a deadly chemical spray.

Another concern is that if Third World countries sympathetic to terrorist groups are empowered with chemical weapons, they might outfit individuals involved in international terrorist activities. Muammar Qaddafi has an extensive history of supporting terrorists, and Saddam Hussein has exhibited similar tendencies. The Iraqi president was in frequent touch with Abu Nidal, who is purported to be among the world's most dangerous terrorists. Intelligence sources also believe that, prior to the Persian Gulf war, Abu Nidal's nephew reopened his uncle's former headquarters in the Iraqi capital of Baghdad. Abu Ibrahim, another international terrorist suspected of bombing aircraft, took up residence there as well. As one U.S. official described Saddam Hussein's probable strategy, "The theory is [that] he wants to have all these tools available. He doesn't care about the public stigma."[12] Following Hussein's defeat in the Persian Gulf war, there was some speculation that terrorists might take revenge through acts in which lethal chemical agents were released.

Chemical weapons have been described as "a terrorist's dream." A medium-sized package "accidentally" left behind in a subway station, railroad terminal, or airport would be sufficient to kill hundreds of people. If a foot-and-a-half-long cylinder of the toxic gas sarin were released through the central air-conditioning system of a large office complex, it is likely that every staff member inside would be dead in a short time.

When asked if he felt Europe was threatened by the possible terrorist use of chemical weapons, François Heisbourg, head of the Institute for Strategic Studies in London, England, replied, "Not yet, but the situation is becoming more disturbing."[13] Others feel there may already be cause for alarm, pointing to the fact that there is no protective shield against what is frequently labeled the poor man's atomic bomb. Since Sweden and Switzerland so far are the only Western nations that have built civilian gas shelters, much of the West remains vulnerable.

Despite pleas from the United Nations and other international bodies, Third World powers that have gone to great lengths to acquire and stockpile chemical weapons do not appear ready to forsake these tools of death. In fact, some Third World countries, resentful of pressure from more powerful nations to abandon their chemical weapons, are quick to point out that Western nations introduced chemical warfare on a far grander scale in World War I. They have also stressed that, after the war, affluent nations sometimes resorted to chemical weaponry when it was advantageous to do so.

Frequently, Third World leaders argue that they can't destroy their chemical-weapons stockpiles as long as their enemies possess nuclear arms. Syria claims that its chemical-weapons program was born in response to Israel's nuclear-warfare capacity. The Syrian foreign minister stated, "We are totally against all weapons of mass destruction: chemical, biological, and nuclear. You cannot disarm one side with one class of weapon and leave the other side to keep its systems intact."[14]

Yet, becoming a chemical-weapons giant is hardly a worthy goal for any country. These weapons are not only morally repugnant to responsible individuals, they have also proven largely ineffective against prepared troops. A Swedish military study concluded that if fighting troops have proper protective clothing and equipment, a chemical-weapons attack would result in only a 5 percent casualty rate. It is estimated that casualties might have even been lower in the Iraq–Iran war if so many of the Iranian soldiers hadn't had thick beards, which prevented their gas masks from fitting properly. According to Seth Carus of the Naval War College Foundation, "Their [chemical weapons] effectiveness is grossly exaggerated in a military sense. What really matters is their deterrent effect."[15]

Part of the problem has to do with the large quantities of gas needed when waging war over a substantial range. In order to annihilate only half of the enemy troops within a square kilometer, either ten tons of mustard gas or four tons of nerve gas would be required. Climate conditions also seriously affect chemical-weapons use. Although mustard gas might linger for a time in the desert heat, some forms of nerve gas would evaporate almost immediately. Affected by wind currents, chemical weapons sometimes blow back on the user and also contaminate land the user hoped to win through battle. Unfortunately, chemical weapons are sometimes most effective when employed against unsuspecting and unprotected civilian populations within targeted areas.

Although aware of the shortcomings, Third World powers are nevertheless not about to dispose of their chemical-weapons arsenals; they have already successfully manipulated the fear value generated by these awesome, if clumsy, instruments of death. Sadly, chemical weapons may be only a hint of threats to come. There is evidence that some Third World powers are in the process of accumulating biological weapons as well.

Before the Persian Gulf war, Iraq had begun to develop lethal germ weapons, capable of eradicating entire cities in a single attack. Iraq's biological-warfare research had been largely conducted in a modern facility at Salman Pak, outside Baghdad, where scientists used the latest Western equipment to produce killer viruses and bacteria.

Saddam Hussein's biological-warfare arsenal was discovered after London officials seized an Iraq-bound shipment of parts for what was purported to be a gigantic cannon capable of firing a shell with a chemical or biological warhead several hundred miles.

At first it was believed that much of Hussein's chemical- and biological-weapons capacity was destroyed during the Persian Gulf war. However, evidence to the contrary has since surfaced. A high-ranking Iraqi scientist who defected to the West revealed that, following the conflict, Hussein grossly misrepresented his remaining chemical- and biological-weapons stockpile to U.N. officials. A significant supply of these lethal agents, along with the missiles for their delivery, remained safely tucked away in secret storage sites throughout Iraq.

Iraq's dubious technological achievements, along with those of other Middle Eastern nations, are a chilling reminder of CIA Director William Webster's warning when he said, "The moral barrier to biological warfare has been breached. At least ten countries are working to produce biological weapons."[16]

# 2

# A KILLING CATALOG: CHEMICAL WEAPONS

Although chemical and biological weapons have long been considered extremely distasteful instruments of war, numerous nations have recently focused both on refining the use of these lethal agents and on stockpiling a variety of them. What was once categorized as an inhumane and unacceptable form of warfare among civilized nations may now be coming into vogue.

Chemical agents are defined as weapons because of their destructive effects on people, animals, or vegetation. A chemical weapon may be a solid, liquid, or gas, and it may consist of a single toxic agent or a combination of benign substances, which, when mixed, become toxic. When unleashed on human beings, chemical weapons affect the nervous system, breathing centers, skin, eyes, nose, and throat as well as other areas of the body. These weapons can be launched against a targeted enemy in a number of ways. Airplanes may either spray an area or drop a bomb containing a chemical agent. Hazardous chemicals may also be fired by artillery, delivered through missile warheads, or released by exploding land mines. The following are some of the better-known chemical weapons and their effects.

**Tear Gas** Although tear gas is more often employed by police officers for riot control than in combative situations between opposing forces, at times it has been relied on for military operations. When used in high concentrations, tear gas causes serious irritation of the respiratory tract and skin. Especially powerful forms of tear gas will also cause severe coughing, as well as nausea. While tear gas is not considered a lethal agent, certain forms of it can temporarily incapacitate unsuspecting combat troops.

Vomiting gas, or adamite, is a virulent type of tear gas. This chemical agent is given its name because it induces intense vomiting in addition to the symptoms common to other tear gases. Vomiting gas, as well as other forms of tear gas, have been used militarily to flush the enemy out of buildings, caves, or other enclosed fortifications.

**Mustard Gas** Actually a liquid spray, mustard gas forms a thick, cloudlike mist, which can linger over an area for days. This garlic-scented chemical agent induces skin and eye irritation, temporary blindness, respiratory difficulties, and large, painful lesions and blisters. When used in high doses, mustard gas causes a significant number of fatalities. Blister gas was perfected by the Russians as a newer, refined version of mustard gas, which was used extensively during World War I. Although blister gas is similar to mustard gas, it is more powerful, tending to completely erode the victim's skin tissue. It is also faster acting than mustard gas.

**Chlorine** Chlorine is a chemical weapon that irritates the nose, throat, and lungs. Its effects include choking and coughing, burning and smarting eyes, and vomiting. A small concentration of chlorine can be lethal, with the victim dying soon after exposure.

**Lewisite** Lewisite is a lethal blistering agent containing arsenic. It enters the victim's body through the skin and lungs. Although lewisite is frequently compared to mustard gas, its effects tend to be more severe. Lewisite's burning and blistering effects begin shortly after exposure. Often victims die within ten minutes.

**Choking Gas** Choking gas, or phosgene, destroys the lining of the body's air passages, resulting in a substantial secretion of mucus in these areas. The mucus blocks the lungs and windpipe, causing the victim to drown in his own fluid secretions. While choking gas was responsible for a large number of casualties during World War I, today it is generally considered inferior to some of the more recently developed chemical weapons.

**Blood Gases** Cyanogen chloride and hydrogen cyanide are chemical agents that affect the blood's capacity to carry oxygen. These fast-acting gases cause choking and suffocation. Cyanogen chloride was first used during World War I, whereas hydrogen cyanide was developed later.

**Nerve Gas** Nerve agents such as tabun, sarin, soman, and VX are colorless, tasteless, odorless, and especially lethal. Nerve gas interrupts the normal flow of nerve impulses, causing a shutdown of essential bodily systems. The victim eventually suffocates as the diaphragm fails to pump the lungs. If nerve gas is either inhaled or absorbed through the skin, its victim can die in less than fifteen minutes.

A single drop of sarin will immediately kill its victim because it paralyzes the nervous system. Tabun is somewhat less toxic but also has the capability to kill quickly. VX, known for its ease in penetrating the skin, is extremely toxic. Unlike the other nerve agents, VX is an oily liquid that retains its deadly potency even after lying on the ground for weeks. Less lethal forms of nerve gas may cause distorted vision and blindness, extremely painful headaches, and other symptoms.

Nerve gas was initially developed in the 1930s as the result of lab work with an unusually potent insecticide. It was later used militarily and by the German SS in Nazi death camps during World War II. Today, considerable quantities of nerve gas are stockpiled by chemical-weapons-producing nations.

**Chemical Defoliants and Anti-crop Weapons** The British first used herbicides as a military tool in World War I. Later, the United States military also employed chemical defoliants and anti-crop weapons to achieve military gains. The wartime value of these measures is described in the U.S. Army manual *Military Biology and Biological Agents,* which states that chemicals possess "high offensive potential for destroying or seriously limiting the production of crops and for defoliating vegetation. . . . There are no proven defensive measures against these compounds. By the time the symptoms appear, nothing can be done to prevent the damage. The compounds are detoxified in the soil after a period of several weeks to several months."

**Agent Orange** Between 1962 and 1971, the U.S. military used chemical agents in the Vietnam War to clear jungle areas thought to conceal enemy Vietcong soldiers. More than 17 million gallons of chemical agents, known as Orange, Blue, and White—named for the colored stripes on their containers—were sprayed over large tracts of land in both South Vietnam and Laos. It is estimated that by the war's end, 368 pounds of chemicals blanketed various combat areas, covering 5 to 15 percent of the region. Before long, the American pilots' unofficial slogan had become "Only We Can Prevent Forests."

Although a 1966 State Department report cited Agent Orange as nontoxic and therefore not harmful to either humans or animals, it has since been learned that the Agent Orange component dioxin is linked to both cancer and birth defects in animals. The presence of dioxin in a compound also intensifies the effects of only mildly carcinogenic (cancer-causing) chemicals.

In one study on the effects of Agent Orange, researchers at the National Cancer Institute checked the records of former Vietnam military dogs against the health files of military dogs that hadn't left the United States. They found that the Vietnam military dogs, exposed to the same chemical sprays inhaled by American service personnel, later developed nearly double the number of benign testicular tumors that other army dogs did. Military dogs serving in Vietnam also had 90 percent more seminomas (malignant tumors of the testes). In addition to the tumor growth, these dogs were one and seven-tenths to two times more vulnerable to various other types of testicular dysfunction.

The researchers noted that the higher occurrence of testicular cancer among Vietnam military canines might be related to the incidence of comparable tumors among Vietnam veterans. As one scientist noted, "The dog is the sentinel model for man."[1]

Unsuspecting military personnel serving in Vietnam had not been instructed to take precautions or to shield themselves from the toxic substance. They swam and bathed in contaminated rivers, ate local food, and drank the water. Some of the servicemen even fashioned crude barbeque pits out of empty Agent Orange barrels.

In the years immediately following the war, there were reports of an increased incidence of cancer in Vietnam. Independent research consistently indicated that this might be related to the extensive Agent Orange sprayings. For example, a Swedish doctor studying industrial health hazards found that workers exposed to the elements in Agent Orange suffered from a higher rate of both Hodgkin's and non-Hodgkin's lymphomas (forms of cancer).

Still another study by the National Cancer Institute involved Kansas farmers who had worked with 2,4-D, a major chemical component in Agent Orange. Farmers who did not wear protective clothing were found to have six times more non-Hodgkin's lymphomas than farmers shielded by a protective covering. An additional indication that the chemical sprays used to strip away Vietnam's jungle cover took their toll on American military personnel came through a number of health studies involving female nurses formerly stationed in Vietnam. Many of these women suffered from a broad range of health problems, which included higher rates of gynecological disorders, more than double the incidence of cancer found in nurses who didn't serve in Vietnam, as well as three times the number of children born with birth defects. It was also noted that twice as many of these ill children died prior to their first birthday. There were other problematic signs as well. Following their husbands' return from the war, an increasing number of Vietnam veterans' wives gave birth to children with severe birth defects.

Although veterans' groups throughout America suspected that a connection existed between the war's chemical defoliation program and the high rate of rare cancers among American service personnel previously stationed in Southeast Asia, the government initially denied that any such parallel existed. Yet, even though lymphoma is a rare form of cancer that generally strikes individuals over fifty years of age, medical centers throughout the country were soon forced to contend with large numbers of significantly younger Vietnam veterans suffering from this formerly unusual disease.

The haunting reality that American service personnel confronted a deadly enemy in Southeast Asia other than the Vietcong was becoming undeniable. As Vietnam veteran Paul Reuterskin, founder of the group Agent Orange Victims International, said before he died after contracting stomach cancer, "I got killed in Vietnam. I just didn't know it at the time."[2]

But despite the substantial number of Vietnam veterans who developed unusual forms of cancer or fathered handicapped children, the government still refused to acknowledge a definitive link between their illnesses and Agent Orange. Both the Reagan and Bush Administrations therefore denied financial compensation to Vietnam veterans for all but a few related health problems.

Although scientists continued to disagree over whether there was a correlation between the illnesses experienced by Vietnam veterans and their exposure to Agent Orange, seven Agent Orange manufacturers, in response to a 1984 suit filed by the American Legion, agreed to pay an out-of-court settlement of 180 million dollars to service personnel who had been exposed to the chemical. It seems that, even prior to its production, some of the manufacturers knew that the herbicide had been linked to birth defects in animals, but they still allowed the product to be commercially marketed. Unfortunately, the monetary settlement did not include an admission of responsibility or even an acknowledgment that Agent Orange contributed to the veterans' subsequent health difficulties. Therefore, to a large degree, the American Legion's original purpose in bringing the lawsuit against the chemical manufacturers was defeated. The veterans' group had sought to establish a traceable link between the Vietnam veterans' ailments and exposure to Agent Orange, to insure that these individuals would be eligible for government compensation.

But, despite the setback, the organization refused to give up. In describing their future intent, an American Legion spokesperson said, "The primary thing we want is for the government to do a study. We consider any diseases caused by Agent Orange the same as getting wounded. It is an injury of war. Agent Orange is a weapon of war."[3]

Ironically, that is exactly what Congress had set out to do a number of years before. After a 1979 series of CBS television documentaries focusing public attention on the harmful effects of Agent Orange, Congress passed a law mandating the Department of Veterans Affairs to undertake a comprehensive study of the chemical's effects. When the department was unable to develop the necessary methodology, the research assignment was transferred to the Atlanta-based Centers for Disease Control (CDC) in 1982. But the work was never completed, and since that time, there have been serious allegations as to why the research project was aborted.

As a result, in the summer of 1990, the American Legion brought its first suit against the federal government since the group's inception in 1919. It charged the government with being remiss in completing its survey of the effects of Agent Orange. A second similar suit was filed by another organization, the Vietnam Veterans of America.

Both lawsuits centered on the controversy over whether the study had been purposely scuttled after five years of ongoing research and an expenditure of 43 million tax dollars. The stakes of the study's outcome were high. Claiming the lack of solid proof, the government stood firm in denying veterans compensation for most health problems associated with Agent Orange. Moreover, research results substantiating the veterans' claims would force the government into a costly policy change. Veteran compensation for just soft-tissue sarcoma and non-Hodgkin's lymphoma—two forms of cancer frequently associated with Agent Orange—would surpass 100 million dollars.

In any case, the government study by the Centers for Disease Control relied on recorded troop movements following area herbicide sprayings to identify military personnel exposed to Agent Orange. Although the army supplied fairly detailed accounts of the soldiers' positions, the research team complained that there were too many gaps in the data. The Environmental Support Group at the Pentagon repeatedly informed the research scientists that daily journals and situation reports were readily available to supplement their information, but CDC still insisted that the overall material was insufficient to arrive at an accurate determination. Deciding that the study wasn't feasible, CDC canceled the project in 1987.

However, an investigation and report by the House Government Operations Committee sharply disagreed with CDC's research findings. This investigation indicated that there was enough information to accurately measure a soldier's exposure to the defoliant. Skeptics serving on the House investigatory committee suspected that CDC was not anxious to highlight factors that might aggravate the Reagan Administration's concern over the substantial amount of money to be paid to veterans if it were found that Agent Orange caused their illnesses. According to the House report:

"The White House was deeply concerned that the Federal Government would be placed in the position of paying compensation to veterans suffering diseases related to Agent Orange, and feared that paying compensation to veterans suffering diseases related to Agent Orange would set a precedent of having the U.S. compensate civilian victims of toxic contaminant exposure too."[4]

Another study that set out to explore the same question further refutes CDC's premise that it is impossible to accurately complete the research. The second study, which was contracted and paid for by the American Legion, was the work of researchers Jeanne Stellman, a public health professor at Columbia University, and her husband, Steven Stellman, assistant health commissioner for biostatistics and epidemiological research for the city of New York.

While the researchers were unable to measure each soldier's precise level of exposure to Agent Orange, they determined that even the likelihood of having been exposed was sufficient to draw significant conclusions about the effect of dioxin on the personnel. As Jeanne Stellman succinctly described their research efforts, "We can evaluate exposure. There are troops [for comparison] who were in areas that were never exposed."[5]

Perhaps among the most outspoken critics of the government's failure to follow through on the 1982 study initiative is former Commander in Chief of Naval Operations Elmo R. Zumwalt, Jr. While head navy commander during the Vietnam War, Zumwalt ordered the use of Agent Orange spray in the Mekong Delta, an area from which enemy Vietcong forces staged devastating ambushes against U.S. patrol boats. Zumwalt hoped the Agent Orange sprayings would destroy the enemy's camouflage and thereby save the lives of navy men.

Undoubtedly, Agent Orange's regional defoliation was instrumental in protecting American sailors from enemy fire. Prior to the herbicide's use, the men had a 6 percent chance of being killed or wounded while patrolling these waters. Following the Agent Orange sprayings, this casualty rate dropped to under 1 percent. At a time when navy personnel were gravely concerned about their chances for survival, Agent Orange greatly eased the men's immediate anxiety. Once the trees were stripped of their leaves and the massive bush growth had vanished, they no longer felt as though they were fighting an invisible enemy. Admiral Zumwalt described his rationale for using the herbicide this way, "[It was] my desire to minimize casualties and end the U.S. involvement in the war as successfully and quickly as possible."

Perhaps one of the cruelest ironies of Zumwalt's order to use a herbicide he believed wasn't harmful to humans was that his son, Elmo Zumwalt III, a lieutenant serving in Vietnam, was among those negatively affected by Agent Orange. When young Elmo returned from the war, he learned he had cancer. Two years later, doctors were shocked to find that Zumwalt was also suffering from a second type of cancer. It was extremely unusual for someone to have non-Hodgkin's lymphoma and then develop Hodgkin's disease.

The odds against Elmo Zumwalt's survival were great, and, unfortunately, one of the few life-extending alternatives available to him was a high-risk bone marrow transplant, which has sometimes been described as one of the most punishing medical procedures known. Zumwalt survived the bone marrow transplant, but the brave young man said that he had "never experienced such physical agony." Although he continued to fight for his life, before long the other form of cancer resurfaced, and in 1988 Elmo Zumwalt III died.

Admiral Zumwalt believes his son's exposure to Agent Orange resulted in the young naval officer's death. In the summer of 1990, when the elder Zumwalt testified before a House subcommittee, he characterized CDC's research efforts to determine the effects of Agent Orange as "a fraud," stating that the agency had done its best to "manipulate and prevent the true facts from being determined." He, along with millions of others, is anxious to see the truth surface.

As of yet, no one can be positive of what the truth will be. Evidence that Agent Orange is deleterious to good health continues to mount. The study involving Kansas farmers linked dioxin, as well as other Agent Orange chemical components, to cancer. In addition, a number of studies of both farmers and victims of industrial accidents in the United States, Italy, Japan, Sweden, and Germany indicate a connection between dioxin and various forms of cancer, as well as porpheria (a liver disease). According to Dr. Arnold Schecter, a professor of preventive medicine at the State University of New York in Binghamton and a consultant to the Massachusetts Agent Orange Program, "The studies are coming together now. I think that new evidence in the past five years shows that Agent Orange—and thus, dioxin—did get into the bodies of some Vietnam veterans. There's evidence based on the Kansas study showing that the components of Agent Orange do cause cancer in humans."[6]

Nevertheless, numerous scientists warn against hastily drawn conclusions. As Peter Kahn, associate professor of biochemistry at Rutgers University and the director of research for the New Jersey State Commission on Agent Orange, stated, "There is plenty of evidence to suggest a connection, but connection is not proof."[7]

However, while waiting for conclusive proof, the veterns recently won some limited gains. In February 1991, the VA awarded disability payments to vets with two forms of cancer, non-Hodgkin's lymphoma and soft-tissue sarcoma. In July, a number of vets who contracted the nerve disorder peripheral neuropathy were also accorded disability payments.

Agent Orange is an example of how use of a chemical weapon may have rebounded back to the user. It is likely that thousands of people suffered serious health problems because of it.

In addition to Agent Orange, the United States isolated and stockpiled other chemical agents to destroy growing vegetation. These include the following anti-crop weapons:

**Wheat Rust** Caused naturally by a fungus *(Puccinia graminis)*, wheat rust can both stunt the growth of vegetation and kill living plants. The fungus forms sturdy spores, which are spread by the wind and thrive in damp, warm climates. The disease is called wheat rust because the fungus causes portions of the affected vegetation to turn reddish brown. If its spread goes unchecked, the resulting plant destruction can be widespread and rapid.

**Rice Blast** In some ways, this plant disease is similar to wheat rust. Rice blast is also a fungus; its spores are carried by the wind; and it does well in warm, rainy regions. When rice blast attacks a rice plant early in its growing cycle, the plant won't bear rice. Although the United States contemplated using rice blast on rice paddies in Southeast Asia during the Vietnam War, it did not follow through on this action.

Chemical defoliants and anti-crop weapons can cause widespread devastation as well as prolonged regional contamination. Unfortunately, the lethal effects of these weapons often continue long after the war in which they were used is over.

# 3
# A KILLING CATALOG: BIOLOGICAL WEAPONS

Biological warfare is the military use of disease-producing microorganisms or their toxins on a designated area to incapacitate or kill people, animals, or vegetation. Biological weaponry may be incorporated into a nation's military strategy in a number of ways. While some biological agents are designed to kill, others merely render the opponents too ill to fight. Still other biological weapons contaminate an enemy's food source, leaving them without further rations and perhaps forcing them to surrender. Most biological weapons are released through the air, but some are also transmitted through water or soil.

Biological weapons often share certain common characteristics. The majority are highly infectious diseases to which the body has no natural immunity. In order to be militarily practical, biological weapons need to be easy and economical to produce; they should also retain their potency outside the laboratory.

Presently there are two available types of biological weapons, "conventional" disease weapons and "designer" disease weapons. Conventional biological weapons isolate diseases that occur naturally in humans and animals to infect a targeted population. Designer biological weapons are diseases specifically created within a laboratory setting, and they are especially difficult to counteract. The following are some of the more commonly discussed conventional biological weapons.

**Anthrax** Although only a few cases of anthrax occur each year in the United States, this often fatal bacterial disease is not uncommon in Africa and other parts of the world. Anthrax typically occurs in animals such as cattle, sheep, and goats. People handling the diseased animals often break out in skin ulcers. Other symptoms may include stomach pain and severe pneumonia. If an infected animal is eaten, intestinal anthrax—for which there is an 80 percent death rate—may occur.

Anthrax is most lethal when its toxins are breathed in. The effect of anthrax bombs falling on a targeted region is extremely deadly. Within hours of inhaling the contaminated air, a victim experiences choking and coughing fits, as well as unusually high fevers. It is soon extremely difficult to breathe. Ninety percent of those affected will not survive the attack. The soil may also be contaminated for over fifty years following an anthrax assault. Gruinard, a small island off the northwest coast of Scotland, is still contaminated as the result of 1942 anthrax testing done there on sheep.

**Q Fever** When occurring naturally, Q fever, which is similar to typhus, is frequently spread through tick bites. Incidence of the disease is somewhat common in cattle, sheep, and other animals. Humans often contract Q fever through handling infected animals or animal waste, inhaling contaminated dust, or drinking milk from an infected animal. Q fever cannot be transmitted from one person to another.

**Tularemia** This disease, which is also known as rabbit fever, is far more common in rodents and other animals than in humans. In nature, tularemia is commonly transmitted through the bite of an infected tick or other insect. Under normal circumstances, humans infected with tularemia have been in contact with an infected animal or have been bitten by a disease-carrying insect.

Individuals stricken with the disease feel extremely weak and listless. They also experience intermittent fever, muscle aches, pain, and chills. If left untreated, disease victims often die.

**Dengue** Also known as breakbone fever or dandy fever, dengue is a contagious viral infection that is transmitted in nature by the same mosquito that spreads yellow fever (see page 47). Although dengue is common in the tropics, it may also occur in temperate climates during the warmer months.

Characteristic symptoms of the malady include fever, headache, exhaustion, and loss of appetite. Soon after contracting the disease, victims experience muscle aches as well as severe pain in the eyes and back. A reddish rash may also appear and last for several days. When employed as a biological weapon, this tropical disease can be easily spread by aerosol spray.

**Botulin** A potent, lethal toxin, botulin is produced by a thick, rod-shaped bacterium known as *Clostridium botulinum*. The microbe does its deadly work when ingested with food that either has not been thoroughly cooked or has been improperly canned or preserved.

The early symptoms, which may appear several hours after eating the contaminated food, include headache, pain, and dizziness. If the condition goes untreated, an individual who has ingested a sufficient quantity of the contaminated food may die from respiratory paralysis in under three days.

Botulin was identified as a dangerous toxin in the late 1700s, when more than a dozen people in a small German town suffered its effects after eating the same contaminated sausage. Today, nearly one hundred people worldwide are affected annually by botulin, with about a quarter of these cases being fatal.

When U.S. scientists first worked on isolating botulin as a biological weapon, they had hoped it could be used in an aerosol spray form to cover a broad area. But when they learned that exposure to direct sunlight eradicates the microbe's toxicity, they explored other methods of delivery.

**Brucellosis** Brucellosis, or undulant fever, is a disease that affects animals such as cattle, goats, wild rabbits, antelope, and caribou. Humans may contract the disease either by drinking milk from an infected animal or through direct contact with the diseased animal or its carcass.

The incubation period, before the early disease symptoms appear, ranges from five days to several months. However, the average incubation time is two weeks. At that point, the person may be feverish as well as fatigued. The exhaustion intensifies as time passes, and over the next few months the infected individual experiences both weight loss and depression. When the U.S. Army began its biological warfare program, brucellosis was studied for its potential weaponry value. But by the 1950s, work on it was abandoned as researchers turned their attention toward faster acting, more predictable diseases.

**Venezuelan Equine Encephalitis (VEE)** First identified in South and Central America, VEE is a disease that may be transmitted to humans and animals by an infected mosquito. Cases of the disease first became apparent in the United States after these mosquitoes traveled across the Rio Grande River into Texas. However, its spread in this country was soon checked as health officials effectively destroyed the insects.

Within hours of being bitten, VEE victims frequently experience high fever and a severe headache. Usually these symptoms fade, and the person recovers in a few days. VEE is more serious in the small percentage of cases in which the disease spreads to the nervous system, but it is only fatal in about 1 percent of infected individuals. During the 1960s, Venezuelan equine encephalitis was among the biological weapons stockpiled by the U.S. Army.

**Plague** The plague is an infection that occurs in rats and other rodents and is transmitted to humans by parasitic fleas from the diseased animals. Symptoms include chills, fever, and swelling of the lymph nodes in the groin and elsewhere.

There are different forms of the plague. The type known as bubonic plague cannot be transmitted from one person to another; it is spread only by fleas from infected rats. On the other hand, pneumonic plague is highly contagious because it can be transmitted through the air by droplets from coughing or even breathing.

During various periods throughout history, plague

epidemics killed thousands of human beings. Good environmental sanitation is an important factor in suppressing this infectious disease. As a biological weapon, this historic killer can be reproduced in either the bubonic or pneumonic form.

**Saxitoxin** Single-celled microscopic plants known as dinoflagellates bloom near many ocean surfaces during the warm-weather months. Sea creatures such as clams, mussels, and oysters ingest these plants. However, dinoflagellates produce a number of harmful substances, including the toxin saxitoxin, which may cause paralysis and even death if the contaminated shellfish are eaten by humans.

The symptoms begin immediately following the meal, as a tingling, burning sensation spreads through the tongue, lips, and cheeks. Paralysis sets in quickly, as the sensation travels outward to the limbs. The throat tightens, and death from suffocation can result within an hour after the respiratory muscles collapse. Toxins extracted from contaminated shellfish have been isolated for their potential use as biological weapons.

**Yellow Fever** Yellow fever, a disease that has been known for centuries, is caused by a virus carried by a mosquito. These infected mosquitoes are most frequently found in the area just below the equator. The virus they carry was probably responsible for many of the deaths among captured Africans brought to America on slave ships over two hundred years ago.

After being bitten by an infected mosquito, a person may not experience any overt symptoms for three days to a week. Following that period, an individual may develop an extremely high temperature, as well as liver dysfunction. The damage to the liver causes the skin to take on a yellowish hue, which is why the disease is called yellow fever. Before the late 1960s, infected mosquitoes were being actively bred to isolate yellow fever as a biological weapon, but since then, more attention has been focused on other diseases believed to have greater warfare potential.

The Defense Department believes further research on biological weapons is necessary because the United States still cannot adequately defend itself against such agents as anthrax. Yet they have acknowledged that these weapons have serious limitations in war. A Defense Department report citing the observations of the Chemical Warfare Review Commission stated that "the very lack of precise control of biological weapons makes their battlefield use less likely, as does the fact that unlike chemical weapons . . . biological agents usually have a period of delay before they take effect."[1]

There are other drawbacks to conventional biological weapons as well. Because most of the disease organisms exist either in humans or animals, they frequently die when exposed to sun, wind, and drastic temperature variations.

More recently, the Defense Department emphasized the importance of current advances in biotechnology that permit the development of unique biological weapons. Through genetic engineering principles, scientists can now create designer weapons, microorganisms capable of causing deadly diseases for which no cures exist. Also, the new techniques can transform previously harmful microorganisms into lethal agents.

In addition to being completely resistant to antibodies and a wide assortment of drugs, designer weapons may also embody the following characteristics:

# A Killing Catalog: Biological Weapons ❏ 49

❏ Increased strength and durability. Designer weapons retain their potency through both long periods of time and sharp temperature changes. This is achieved by means of microencapsulation, a process by which biological organisms are shielded from injurious elements while encased within organic compounds. In addition to increasing weapon potency, this process has greatly broadened the range of possible diseases that might be employed as instruments of biological warfare.

❏ More lethal. Through genetic engineering techniques, disease organisms used as biological weapons can be made faster acting as well as more lethal.

❏ Efficient production. The U.S. Army reports that advances in biotechnology have dramatically reduced the amount of time and factory space necessary to produce specifically tailored biological weapons.

❏ Greater virulence than chemical weaponry. Enhancements achieved through biotechnology are expected to yield specially developed neurotoxic weapons that are hundreds of times more deadly than any nerve gas currently in existence.

U.S. researchers are working diligently to devise effective defenses against such potentially devastating weaponry. Although the 1972 Biological and Toxin Weapons Convention Treaty prohibits developing, producing, and storing biological weapons except for defensive purposes, it "does not preclude research into those offensive aspects of biological agents necessary to determine what defensive measures are required."[2] As an infectious disease specialist from Salt Lake City, Utah, said, "It's like testing a vest against bullets. You first need to have the bullets."[3]

The impressive advances and refinements in biological weaponry have focused significant attention on a once unpopular military alternative. As a former Deputy Assistant Secretary of Defense for Negotiations Policy testified before Congress, "The prevailing judgment of years ago that biological warfare is not militarily significant is now quite unsustainable. Biological warfare can be designed to be effective across the spectrum of combat, including special operations and engagements at a tactical level."[4]

Perhaps among the most unsettling aspects of the recent biological-warfare advances are the speed and minimal cost at which these weapons can be mass-produced. Such weapons are also sufficiently compact to be carried in a pocket or purse. Their effects are indistinguishable from those of diseases occurring from natural causes, unless special monitoring is performed prior to their release on the targeted area. Intelligence sources also stress that production facilities for designer biological weapons can be easily camouflaged, making them especially difficult to pinpoint.

According to a Defense Department report:

"While the discovery and development of these tools required extraordinarily skilled and 'leading edge' scientists, the application of such tools has become routine work delegated in many cases to persons having minimal technical training. . . . Biological warfare is not new, but it has a new face."[5]

# 4
# EARLY DEVELOPMENTS

Various forms of chemical and biological warfare have characterized human conflicts for centuries. Over two thousand years ago, Greeks and Romans used decaying corpses to poison their enemy's drinking water. The militaristic Spartans of Greece devised an early form of poison gas by burning sulfur and pitch to send dense clouds of sulfur dioxide over their foe's cities.

Although militarily effective, even in early times, such methods were often perceived as morally repugnant. While Julius Caesar sometimes relied on primitive chemical and biological weapons in expanding the Roman Empire, Roman justices condemned the use of such weaponry, stating that "war is waged with arms, not poison."

Various types of chemical and biological weapons have also played a role in hostile confrontations in America. During the French and Indian War, Lord Jeffrey Amherst, the British commander in chief in the American colonies, relied on an early form of biological warfare to wipe out a group of rebellious American Indians. In 1763 Amherst gave two blankets and a handkerchief used by soldiers who had died of smallpox as a gift to the unsuspecting Ohio Potawatomi Indian tribe. The gesture resulted in a widespread tribal smallpox epidemic that cost many lives.

During the Civil War, Confederate troops used the decaying remains of dead animals to poison the drinking water of Union soldiers. In response, Union forces contemplated launching an artillery shell filled with chlorine (a deadly agent later used in World War I).

Pace-setting technological developments following the Civil War caused some concern that possible advances in chemical and biological warfare might eventually result in widespread human suffering. Concerned leaders from around the globe met on a number of occasions to design and implement policies to prohibit this distasteful means of waging war.

Their efforts resulted in the First International Peace Conference, held in The Hague in 1899. There, in the interest of protecting humankind, nations agreed to "abstain from the use of projectiles, the object of which is the diffusion of asphyxiating or deleterious gases."[1] Interestingly, although U.S. representatives participated in the international conference, American military leaders remained staunch in their opposition to restraining the use of chemical warfare. As a result, America was among the few nations in attendance that refused to sign the policy.

Yet it was not the United States that soon afterward violated the spirit of the ban by launching the largest scale chemical-weapons attack ever experienced on earth. Instead, Germany manipulatively skirted the agreement's language to employ poison gas against its opposition in World War I. On April 22, 1915, German soldiers secretly placed nearly six thousand cylinders of liquid chlorine in trenches along a four-mile stretch in Flanders Field near the Belgian town of Ypres. The Germans' subsequent use of heavy artillery on the trenches splintered the cylinders, releasing the lethal gas into the air.

Early Developments ❑ 53

The First International Peace Conference specifically banned the use of chemical "projectiles," but, as the Germans shattered cylinders to disperse the poison, they contended that they hadn't violated the agreement. Although the German government technically defended its position, it was more difficult to do so morally.

Germany's opposition was devastated by the attack. In less than a day, five thousand French soldiers were killed, while another ten thousand were seriously wounded following the chemical-weapons assault. Survivors did not suffer a benign fate. An observer later described them as follows: "Faces, arms, [and] hands were a shiny gray-black. With mouths open and lead-glazed eyes, they were all swaying backwards and forwards, trying to get their breath, struggling, struggling for life."[2]

Meanwhile, German scientists perfected mustard gas, which the German military used in 1917 in a second attack on Ypres. Sometimes referred to as the "king of gas," mustard gas was considered to be the most potent World War I chemical weapon. When the mustard shells were released, Allied soldiers initially detected only a garlic-scented odor permeating the air. Unaware of what was to come, some even ignored the attack. Yet within hours, the same troops were plagued by large, painful blisters, blindness, choking, and death within the ranks.

Although seemingly appalled that such a brutal form of warfare was used so callously, Allied forces soon prepared themselves for comparable retaliation. "I am not pleased with the idea of poisoning men. Of course, the entire world will rage about it at first, and then imitate us,"[3] predicted one German eyewitness following his country's first chemical onslaught.

Throughout the Allies' direct and forceful retaliation, both sides continued to develop increasingly effective chemical-weapons combinations. Technicians also quickly devised enhanced protective gear for soldiers subjected to enemy gas attacks in the field. At first crude flannel coverings soaked in a baking soda solution were used, but before long, modernized gas masks were issued to the military.

By the war's end, a total of approximately 124,000 tons of chemicals was used by both sides on battlefields. Nearly 92,000 people died as the result of poison gas during the conflict, while an additional 1,300,000 casualties were reported.

Yet, despite the horror of chemical weapons, following the fighting, military personnel in a number of countries urged their governments to continue enhancing this weaponry. In America, the U.S. Chemical Corps enticed outstanding scientists to work for them by appealing to their sense of patriotism. By 1918, the forty-million-dollar Edgewood Arsenal in Maryland employed twelve hundred researchers and technicians to refine and produce new chemical weapons. The work done at Edgewood and other similar facilities around the world ushered chemical weapons into a new age of sophistication.

However, at the same time, the sight of recovering gassed soldiers returning home to the United States from the war provoked a loud public outcry for a firm ban against the future use of chemical weapons. This time, the U.S. assumed a leading role in pushing for a new international policy to insure that the World War I gassings never be repeated.

The result of these efforts was the 1925 Geneva Protocol. The Protocol outlaws the use of biological weapons and prohibits "the use in war of asphyxiating, poisonous, or other gases, and of all liquids, materials, and devices."[4] Eventually, 129 nations signed the pact. Even those that declined to do so were not expected to escape repercussions if they violated the agreement, since these measures were now regarded as an accepted aspect of international conduct. Ironically, although the United States signed the Protocol and had helped to initiate negotiations for it, it did not officially ratify the treaty until decades later, in 1975.

There have been a number of documented violations of the 1925 Geneva Protocol. One was Italy's use of mustard gas in Ethiopia in 1935–1936, followed by Japan's attack on China with mustard gas and other chemical and biological agents between 1937 and 1945. The Japanese also conducted biological warfare experiments on prisoners of war and others during World War II. The United States sprayed large tracts of jungle terrain with Agent Orange and other herbicides from 1962 to 1971 during the Vietnam conflict, and Iraq used mustard gas and possibly other chemical agents against both Iran and its own Kurdish population during the 1980s' Iraq–Iran war. Although there have been other accusations of Protocol violations by various nations, so far the lack of valid documented evidence in these instances makes it impossible to say with certainty that they have transpired.

There has also been some debate surrounding the Geneva Protocol's interpretation. The United States asserts that the use of herbicides (such as those it employed during the Vietnam War) and some riot-control agents, such as tear gas, are not covered under the Protocol. Britain concurs that the use of basically nontoxic riot-control agents is not in violation of the Protocol and has used this form of gas during confrontations in its conflict with northern Ireland. In 1966, the U.S. delegate at the First Committee of the United Nations General Assembly explained U.S. thinking when he said that the Protocol "does not apply to all gases, and it certainly does not prohibit the use of simple tear gas. . . . It is unreasonable to contend that any rule or international law prohibits the use in military combat against an enemy of nontoxic chemical agents that governments around the world commonly use to control riots by their own people."[5]

Following the international ban on chemical warfare initiated by the Geneva Protocol, a number of nations began to seriously assess their biological-weapons capabilities. The Protocol also prohibited using biological weapons but did not limit research and weapons stockpiling for defensive purposes. The United States had a special committee of outstanding scientists, appointed by the National Academy of Science, submit a report to the U.S. secretary of war with their recommendations for research in this area. The scientists concurred that U.S. residents, livestock, and crops were extremely vulnerable to an enemy attack with biological weapons. In addition to recommending such defensive measures as developing vaccines and protective systems for our water supply, the report also insinuated that the government might wish to begin its own research on the offensive use of biological weaponry.

As the United States entered World War II, the nation's blatant weakness in this area was especially unsettling to top-ranking military personnel, who seriously doubted that aggressor nations would adhere to the Geneva Protocol when the stakes were so high. Heeding the scientists' warning, in April 1942, Secretary of War Henry L. Stimson sent a memo to President Roosevelt in which he stated that, as far as biological weapons were concerned, "We must be prepared." Yet Stimson advised caution in this endeavor, adding, "And the matter must be handled with great secrecy and vigor."[6] Acknowledging to the president that "biological warfare is dirty business," the secretary of war felt it would be wise to have civilian professionals monitor the army's research in this area. As he explained his intent to President Roosevelt, "Entrusting the matter to a civilian agency would help in preventing the public from being unduly concerned over any ideas that the War Department might be contemplating the use of this weapon offensively."[7]

The new research division, blandly named the War Research Service (WRS), began its work with a budget of two hundred thousand dollars and the hope of soon broadening its base. Within a short period of time, clandestine research operations on biological weaponry were being conducted on twenty-eight American university campuses. These included such prestigious educational institutions as Harvard University, Columbia University, Cornell University, the University of Chicago, Stanford University, and the University of Notre Dame.

As World War II progressed, research on biological weapons expanded greatly. The army received millions of dollars to erect new research facilities in areas other than college campuses. Among the largest of these was the thirteen-million-dollar research lab at Fort Detrick in Frederick, Maryland. A number of outstanding scientists were recruited to staff the substantially expanded network. In appraising the urgency of the task at hand, one microbiologist said, "The likelihood that bacterial warfare will be used against us will surely be increased if an enemy suspects that we are unprepared to meet it and return it blow for blow."[8]

Among the weapons the United States hoped to develop for its World War II biological-warfare arsenal were deadly five-hundred-pound anthrax bombs and laboratory-produced botulin, both of which are lethal agents. But things did not go as planned. Because the necessary research and assembly had not proceeded with sufficient speed, by 1944 United States scientists had only produced a few bombs, which had not even been tested. At that point, it was clear that a retaliatory attack by the U.S. with biological weapons was out of the question.

In an effort to disguise our vulnerability in this area, over one hundred thousand American soldiers were inoculated against botulin. The military hoped this ploy would trick the opposition into believing that the U.S. already possessed an ample arsenal of biological weapons and was merely vaccinating its soldiers to protect them during possible retaliation measures. Actually, the diversion was nothing more than a high-risk bluff. If the Germans used biological weapons, American forces probably would have responded defensively with gas.

However, although the Germans didn't know it, if they had resorted to chemical weapons, the United States might have been far outflanked. This was due to advances in chemical warfare achieved by the Germans only a few years prior to the outbreak of World War II. Ironically, German scientists accidentally stumbled onto a chemical many times more toxic than their most potent war gas. The newly discovered chemical killer was nerve gas, and in a short time German chemists refined and stockpiled several virulent forms of this lethal agent.

Yet, as it turned out, the extensive funding and research channeled into developing biological weapons to fight Hitler's forces were unnecessary. While the Allies feared the Germans might load the missile warheads of their powerful V-1 "buzz bombs" with biological or chemical agents, only conventional explosives were ever used. And although Hitler relied on poison gas to equip the death chambers of Nazi concentration camps, neither chemical nor biological weapons were employed against enemy troops during the war.

It is not known why Hitler discontinued research on biological agents and banned the use of Germany's newly developed nerve gases. His reasons, though, could have been related to his personal World War I experience, when, as a soldier, he had been temporarily blinded by a blast of mustard gas. Adolf Hitler wrote of the incident, "My eyes had turned into glowing coals; it had grown dark around me."

Perhaps surprisingly, England, rather than Germany, seriously contemplated resorting to chemical weapons during World War II after German aerial bombings took a serious toll on several British cities. In a top-secret memo, Winston Churchill wrote:

"It is absurd to consider morality on this topic when everybody used it in the last war without a word of complaint from the moralists or the Church. On the other hand, in the last war the bombing of open cities was regarded as forbidden. Now everybody does it as a matter of course. It is simply a question of fashion changing as she does between long and short skirts for women.

"We could drench the cities of the Ruhr and many other cities in Germany in such a way that most of the population would be requiring constant medical attention. . . . I want the matter studied in cold blood by sensible people."[9]

Fortunately, Churchill's close advisors judiciously persuaded the English prime minister to abandon the plan, as they believed such an action might both prolong the war and provoke a virulent counterattack.

Although biological and chemical weapons were not used by Allied and Axis powers during World War II in Europe, there is evidence to suggest that the Japanese employed chemical weapons against both Chinese troops and civilians during the war. Records kept by the Chinese army indicate that a minimum of two thousand Chinese were killed by chemical weapons, while an additional thirty-five thousand people suffered injuries. Japan's use of mustard gas against the Chinese was further verified in a document titled "Japanese Gas Warfare in China," presented by China's ambassador to England at the Pacific War Council in London in 1942. According to this report:

"Japanese planes in relays of threes and fives also participated in a gas attack, dropping more than three hundred bombs. The area thus gassed was crowded with Chinese civilians, prohibited by the Japanese from evacuating when the Chinese began to counterattack. The types of gas used then were tear, sneezing, and mustard gas, which caused many fatalities."

There are also documents that detail Japan's use of Chinese POWs as human guinea pigs in various World War II weapon studies. Substantial incriminating data demonstrate that experiments in both biological and chemical warfare were conducted. This includes recovered records that recount the effects of mustard gas experiments on sixteen Chinese prisoners. The prisoners were divided into individual units and given various types of clothing to wear. While some prisoners had gas masks, others had neither gas masks nor shoes. The different prisoners were also confined in special areas for the duration of the experiments. A portion of the prisoners remained locked in a building, some were kept in underground shelters, and others were left under a flimsy machine gun cover.

A total of 9,800 shells of mustard gas were fired at the Chinese POWs throughout the four-day test period. The following is an excerpt from the test results report. It describes the condition of Prisoner 513, who had been exposed to the gas while shielded under a light cover without a gas mask.

"10:00 A.M.: September 12th—headache; fatigue, heart acceleration; body temperature 38 degrees; skin, particularly facial skin, becomes pitch black in color, and all blisters are covered with scabs; shoulders are inflamed and many big blisters are scattered over them; on the abdomen there are many tiny white scabs; misty eyes and eye irritation; trouble with eyesight; constant tears . . . eye mucus; running nose, hoarse voice; croup; phlegm; . . . pain and oppressive sensation in the chest and cardiac dullness."[10]

The report did not specify the eventual fate of prisoner 513 or any other prisoner in the study.

Apparently, Japan also conducted germ-warfare experiments on American and British prisoners of war captured in the Pacific. At a hearing on September 17, 1986, before the House Committee on Veterans Affairs, Subcommittee on Compensation, Pension, and Insurance, Frank James, POW #1268, an American soldier who had been captured by the Japanese during World War II, related his experiences:

"I was one of those POWs captured by the Japanese armed forces after the fall of Bataan and Corregidor in the Philippines during the early part of 1942. Of the Americans captured, fifteen hundred were moved by ship in 1942 from the Philippines to Manchuria (China). This group was joined en route in Korea by some British and Australian soldiers captured in Singapore."

The facility the POWs were taken to in the Manchurian city of Mukden contained three brick buildings and a hospital. The entire complex was surrounded by both a high brick wall and an electrified fence. As Frank James continued to describe his stay in the POW facility:

"Upon arrival at Mukden on November 11, 1942, we were met by a team of medical personnel wearing masks. They sprayed liquid in our faces, and we were given injections. We were subjected to having a glass probe inserted in our rectums. This group left the camp and returned only two more times to my knowledge."

Over three hundred Allied POWs died that winter, although at the time the other prisoners didn't know the cause of their deaths. Instead of being cremated, their bodies were retained until the Japanese medical team returned with an autopsy table and a supply of specimen jars. James recounted the circumstances:

"The table was installed in the building where the dead were stored, and two POWs were selected to work with the team. I was one of those men. Our duties were to lift the bodies that had been selected off the table. These had been identified by a tag tied to the big toe, which listed the POW's number. The Japanese then opened the bodies and took out the desired specimens, which were placed into containers, marked with the POWs' numbers and taken away by the Japanese medical group."[11]

James was not aware of why certain bodies were selected for autopsies or how these choices related to the previous sprayings, injections, and probings. Fortunately, Frank James survived both the war and the experiments performed on him. However, even years after returning home, he still suffers from such serious health problems as emphysema, diabetes, arteriosclerosis, hearing loss, loss of sensation in his extremities, and heart problems.

Numerous other POWs who survived the prisoner-of-war camp at Mukden have experienced serious medical problems as well. Yet at the war's end these POWs were advised not to speak about their experiences as participants in Japan's biological warfare experiments. There may have been a dual reason why officials were anxious to suppress news of these events. Some believe the United States wanted to establish friendly relations with its former enemy following the war. It was also rumored that the United States granted Japanese scientists involved in the germ warfare experiments immunity from war criminal prosecution in return for the data they had collected.

To create these lethal agents of war, the Japanese established a top-secret chemical-weapons facility on the tiny island of Okunoshima in the inland sea that divides Japan's mainland. During World War II, the Japanese erased the tiny island from even the most detailed maps of Japan to insure strict confidentiality regarding the plant's purpose and stockpiling capacity.

New employees at the chemical-weapons facility were required to take an oath of secrecy regarding their work. Security was so strenuously enforced that staff members were not even permitted to discuss their assigned daily tasks with family members. To insure that regulations were strictly adhered to, military police conducted unannounced visits to homes, where they vigorously questioned the staff's families to ascertain how much they knew. Military police disguised as workers also observed employees at the plant and monitored their conversations.

From 1937 to 1944, the chemical plant functioned at optimum capacity. For many months, the facility remained in operation twenty-four hours a day, while alternating shifts of employees. During such peak periods, as many as five to six thousand people worked there. Near the war's end, when there was an acute shortage of manpower, both women and children were recruited to help the war effort by staffing the plant.

As it turned out, many of these workers suffered comparable fates to those on whom the deadly chemical weapons were eventually used. As worker safety precautions were not a top priority at the plant, staff members were continually exposed to gas leaks during their eleven- to thirteen-hour shifts. Plant work areas were so heavily contaminated that the staff was instructed to watch the caged parakeets placed in the rooms with them. If a gas leak worsened and the small bird toppled over dead, the workers moved to another area of the plant for a time.

But these minimal efforts did little to help the workers, who suffered varying degrees of exposure to poisonous agents on a daily basis. It is estimated that at least two-thirds of the staff were adversely affected. Numerous workers who had experienced vision problems later went blind, and a carpenter who injured his finger mending a bombshell used to deliver poison gas died three days after the incident.

Perhaps the most widespread symptom among the workers was the inflammation that appeared around their hips, armpits, and genitals. Although the staff was provided with masks, these shields were somewhat ineffective. Before long, the poison's effect was also visible on the workers' faces, which began to turn purple or black.

Even though there was a hospital building on the island, the treatment provided was grossly inadequate in view of the workers' plight. Employees visiting the hospital had their eyes washed and throats cleansed with a mild spray. Medicated compresses were applied to their necks, and, before being sent back to work at the factory, they were told to take several baths every day and to generously powder the irritated areas of their bodies.

It is likely that women at the plant suffered the worst effects of the poison gas. Although both male and female workers wore only partially effective gas masks, the masks were designed for men, and their loose fit on many of the women allowed the poison gas to seep through more easily. Within a short period of time, female employees began to spit up blood and faint at their work stations.

Before long, chemical refuse and gas escaping from the plant polluted the small island on which the factory stood. People who had never been inside the plant but who worked on the island burning rubbish, cutting grass, and piling up boxes were also forced to breathe in the contaminated air and subsequently became ill. Students from the Adanoumi Pacific Girls High School, sent to the island to help the war effort, later recalled that by the time they arrived, the trees were withered and it was impossible to escape the foul stench that permeated the island.

Many workers who remained well while working at

the plant hoped they had escaped the poison's harmful effects. But often this wasn't so. After the war, individuals who spent time on Okunoshima Island suffered from a disproportionate incidence of lung and stomach cancer, chronic bronchitis, and a number of other ailments.

# 5
# "TRUST BUT VERIFY"

Following World War II, the United States continued to develop and stockpile biological weapons. Nevertheless, during much of that time, the U.S. frequently asserted that biological weapons were inappropriate tools in conventional warfare because they were unpredictable, slow-working, and exceedingly difficult to limit precisely to the targeted area. There was always the danger that a disease used to kill enemy soldiers might spread to allied troops or the civilian population. After declaring in 1969 that such volatile agents "may produce global epidemics," President Richard Nixon promised to halt further biological-weapons development as well as destroy already existing stockpiles.

Perhaps an even more binding step in this direction came in 1972, when the United States, along with numerous other nations, signed the Biological and Toxin Weapons Convention Treaty. According to this agreement, nations are forbidden to develop, produce, or accumulate biological agents except for defensive purposes. The treaty did not address the issue of chemical weapons because these agents are covered under the Geneva Protocol of 1925. However, plans were initiated to devise an updated companion ban on chemical agents.

Although the convention's intent was laudable, many believed the new treaty was practically doomed from its inception, as the document was severely flawed. It lacked concrete measures to insure compliance, there were no established channels through which to resolve conflicts, and the treaty's ambiguous language failed to clearly delineate offensive as opposed to defensive research.

Yet, at first, the United States largely complied with the treaty's intent. As production of chemical weapons ceased, arsenals of U.S. biological agents were destroyed. But although chemical and biological weapons seemed to have taken a backseat for a time, they were hardly erased from the minds of military strategists. Intermittent studies conducted throughout much of the 1970s determined that, if forced to do so, the United States remained ill equipped to defend against a Soviet biological weapons attack. In addition, before long, the military's interest in chemical warfare again peaked, as the development of new binary chemical weapons appeared to eliminate many of the safety hazards formerly associated with this war tool.

Though Pentagon officials in the mid-1970s continually warned of the upper hand maintained by the Soviets in this realm, President Jimmy Carter hesitated to take the necessary action to even up the odds; he feared that revitalizing chemical-weapons production efforts would disrupt ongoing international negotiations for a new chemical-weapons treaty. Earlier, President Gerald Ford had also resisted similar advice from defense strategists.

Although an air of uncertainty and unpreparedness now permeated the atmosphere, by the time President Ronald Reagan took office in 1980, the groundwork for change had been laid. Reagan perceived the Soviet buildup in both chemical and biological weapons as an imminent threat to the national security. During the president's early years in office, he raised the budgetary allotments for chemical- and biological-weapons (CBW) programs. He also emphasized to Congress that the U.S. could no longer afford to forestall the production of new chemical weapons.

The administration believed it was imperative for the United States to strengthen its position as a leading military power. Reagan firmly maintained that, although an eventual international ban on both chemical and biological weapons was desirable, it could never be achieved unless the United States first matched the military prowess of the Soviet Union. Ironically, the Reagan Administration determined that it was crucial to manufacture new chemical weapons before discarding them.

These sentiments resulted in a dramatic broadening of both our chemical- and biological-weapons programs. In 1985 when Reagan appointed a Chemical Warfare Review Commission, the group's findings supported the notion that the United States would be forced to either surrender or resort to nuclear war if the Soviets attacked using their substantial chemical-weapons arsenal. The commission recommended that the United States instead initiate the rapid development of binary chemical weapons, along with new delivery systems to insure their effectiveness.

The administration also repeatedly emphasized to both Congress and the media that, since the Soviets had either violated or in various ways skirted previous bans on biological and chemical weapons, their present stockpiles were now a deadly threat to peace. A Defense Department report to the House of Representatives indicted the Soviet Union for actively violating the 1972 Biological and Toxin Weapons Convention on a number of occasions, including the use of yellow rain, or sprayed toxins, in Southeast Asia and the deployment of chemical weapons in Afghanistan. It also stated that the U.S.S.R. had been "using the capabilities of genetic engineering to create novel weapons."[1]

There has been some speculation as to whether the Soviet Union is actually guilty of all it has been accused of. A great deal of controversy resulted over U.S. claims that Soviet-supported troops in Southeast Asia resorted to using yellow rain. According to U.S. government reports, the toxin attacks occurred when aircraft showered specific regions with a poisonous yellow substance, which fell to the ground, causing serious health problems as well as killing large numbers of villagers.

As the investigation of these allegations broadened to include independent organizations both inside and outside the United States, much of the evidence on which the U.S. government based its original claims was found to be faulty. Researchers from Britain, Australia, Canada, France, Thailand, and the United States analyzed samples of the powdery yellow splashes purported to be yellow rain. But, when placed under an ordinary microscope, the "yellow rain" samples were shown to consist largely of pollen! The pollen concentration of the various internationally tested samples was nearly identical. The researchers concluded that the pollen level was far too high for it to have collected naturally in the surrounding environment. The puzzle was how the high pollen level had accumulated.

The conclusion that the chemical weapon yellow rain was actually only pollen deposits placed the government in an embarrassing position. In response, the administration argued that Soviet scientists had probably purposely added pollen to the toxic mixture to better disguise its true content. An army medical intelligence analyst suggested that the combination was a "very clever mixture," since once the spray dried, the wind could easily cast the toxic substance about, to be inhaled by unsuspecting victims in the vicinity. Yet this theory was not credible because previously tested samples of yellow rain had remained dormant rather than dispersing easily.

Furthermore, when independent scientists, who found it curious that pollen was present in every sample of "yellow rain" analyzed, asked how this could have occurred, the U.S. Deputy Assistant Secretary of State for Politico-Military Affairs answered, "I have no idea how the Soviets produce this stuff. We've not been in their factory."[2] Despite continued U.S. government assertions that the Soviets had devised a deadly poison, many scientists throughout the world found it increasingly difficult to believe that the Russians actually collected vast quantities of honeybee pollen to enhance their chemical weaponry.

Yet a nagging question still remained. If the deposited pollen wasn't a component of a Soviet chemical agent, then what was it? The answer, which eventually came from a honeybee expert at Yale University, served to dispel previous allegations. Yellow rain proved not to be a chemical weapon, but was instead a physiological component of the bee's digestive system—the powdery yellow deposits were nothing more than the feces of wild honeybees.[3] Further testing of the substance revealed that the chemical agent previously thought to be present in the droppings could not be found even in large amounts of the deposits. Once incoming data from various sources confirmed this conclusion, scientists realized that little was known about the behavior of the tropical Asian honeybee. They were anxious to learn whether these bees defecated together while flying in groups and therefore might produce a shower of fecal matter, which could have been mistaken for an aircraft's deadly chemical spray.

As anticipated, when this phenomenon was investigated by two independent United States scientists and a Thai colleague, the trio discovered that wild honeybees, flying at levels too high to be easily discerned from the ground, did defecate collectively. These droppings frequently fell for several minutes at a time, often dotting an area as large as an acre with yellow drops.

Another incident that raised a great deal of concern over possible Soviet violations of the 1972 biological-weapons treaty was the mysterious anthrax epidemic, occurring in April 1979 in the Soviet city of Sverdlovsk. The U.S. Defense Department alleged that the outbreak was the result of an accident at a nearby secret biological-weapons facility. According to the Department's report:

"An accidental release of anthrax occurred within the Microbiology and Virology Institute in Sverdlovsk City, after a pressurized system probably exploded. It was estimated that the accident resulted in one thousand or more anthrax cases."[4]

The Soviets denied U.S. charges, claiming that the epidemic was due to the ingestion of tainted meat purchased illegally by the epidemic victims on the black market. They stressed that the effects of ingesting anthrax spores differed from those of inhaling the contaminant, as would occur in an explosion. Nevertheless, the U.S. Defense Department clung to its suspicions.

To convince both the United States government and U.S. scientists, three prestigious Soviet scientists presented a detailed report on the anthrax outbreak. Speaking before an assembly of scientists and journalists at the Johns Hopkins School of Hygiene and Public Affairs in Maryland, as well as at medical centers in Washington, D.C., and Cambridge, Massachusetts, the Soviets provided slides of the intestinal anthrax, which had taken the lives of some stricken Soviet citizens. Petr Burgasov, the Soviet deputy minister of health, stressed that there were just ninety-six incidents of anthrax, out of which sixty-four had been fatal. In an emotional plea to the audience, he said, "I would like very much that you take my word for this and exclude the fantasy that thousands of people fell ill. What else do you need for proof? I don't understand your doubts at all."[5]

Yet, despite what might have been the best of intentions, the Soviet scientists were unable to indisputably prove their story. The U.S. government remained unconvinced, and independent scientists attending the forum indicated that they would have liked to see more data. However, some researchers were willing to give the Soviet scientists the benefit of the doubt. One well-known U.S. scientist, formerly with the federal Centers for Disease Control in Atlanta, Georgia, stated, "Their epidemiology is somewhat different from ours, somewhat less rigorous and more argumentative, but they told a consistent story, they seem to be sincere, and they deserve our full attention. This is not proof, but I've lived long enough to know that proof is a very elusive thing."[6]

Meanwhile, the doubts created by what may or may not have been an innocent episode only served to fuel feelings of military vulnerability in the United States. Pentagon officials insisted that, since it was impossible to verify whether various nations adhered to the treaty, it was imperative that the U.S. act to create a biological-weapons defense strategy. With this strategy, the U.S. could counter the perceived growing threat from the Soviet Union, other nations, and terrorist groups who might eventually possess these weapons. Some believed that the recent rapid developments in genetic engineering and biotechnology raised the stakes even higher.

In response, Congress appropriated substantial allocations for defense spending in this realm. In 1980, at the start of President Ronald Reagan's first term in office, there hadn't been any expenditures for research and development in biotechnology. But by 1987, funding for these measures climbed to one hundred and nineteen million dollars. In fact, by the late 1980s, scientists from government, college, and corporate laboratory facilities in over one hundred sites around the country were actively working on both biological- and chemical-weapons research projects. Although their efforts might appear to be in direct violation of treaty bans on biological and chemical weapons, the U.S. Defense Department justified its right to proceed on the grounds that the research was defensive and therefore crucial to our national security in the event of a biological- or chemical-warfare attack.

Even though the United States observed a self-imposed moratorium on chemical-weapons production from 1969 to 1987, it didn't take long to build up a substantial arsenal of these deadly agents. By 1989, America was believed to have stockpiled over thirty thousand tons of chemical weapons. The American Chemical Society estimates that the amount is sufficient to annihilate the world's population five thousand times over. Yet, in spite of the extensive stockpiling, tensions in some sectors were heightened by the rumor that the Soviet Union possessed ten times that amount.

To worsen matters, all had not gone as planned in producing the Big Eye bomb, which was to have been the shining star of the enhanced chemical-weapons program. Ideally, the Big Eye would have the capacity to immobilize large tracts of enemy territory with its potent delivery of the toxic nerve agent VX. But the Big Eye was never fully perfected because its development was impeded through the years by an assortment of technical difficulties.

While the weapons buildup continued, progress slowed on international efforts to arrive at an updated chemical-weapons ban. However, use of chemical weapons in the Iraq–Iran war set the stage for the 1980s formation of the Australia group. Led by Australia, this band of nineteen industrial nations (including the U.S.) hoped to stop the proliferation of chemical weapons by uniformly establishing national export controls on this type of weaponry, as well as on agents generally needed in the production of chemical weapons. The group compiled a list of the chemicals most likely to be used to manufacture dangerous weapons and urged chemical corporations within their own borders to reject business offers that might possibly be linked to chemical-weapons development in Iraq, Iran, Syria, and Libya.

The Australia group also shares information on chemical-weapons proliferation, as it seeks new ways to inhibit the use of chemical weapons. The organization does not have a constitution or charter, and its agreements are not binding by international law. Although its purpose is admirable, unfortunately, many nations that are intent on acquiring chemical weapons still manage to do so.

Yet, the Australia group's impact was strengthened in March 1991, when the Bush Administration tightened U.S. export regulations on materials used in chemical and biological weapons and their missile-delivery systems. The list of controlled substances was expanded from eleven to fifty. These new regulations also apply to "dual use" chemicals and equipment, which have legitimate peacetime value.

While the U.S. effectively improved domestic controls, it had been less successful in devising an acceptable U.S.–Soviet plan to reduce chemical-weapons stockpiles. Superpower negotiations were especially hampered by the disagreement over verification procedures. But while the Soviets previously resisted U.S. demands for on-site inspections, they later agreed to accept any checking system the U.S. desired. Yet a firm agreement was not around the corner. The Reagan Administration had demanded that any ban on chemical weapons be global, insisting that the elimination of this weaponry by the superpowers would only afford smaller nations a dangerous edge. Reagan also felt it essential that the ban agreed upon incorporate foolproof verification methods. The phrase "trust but verify" was commonly heard.

Nevertheless, various attempts at further negotiations continued. One hundred and forty-nine nations met in Paris from January 7–11, 1989, to participate in the Conference on the Prohibition of Chemical Weapons. Attending nations reaffirmed their commitment to the 1925 Geneva Protocol and acknowledged the importance of continuing talks to devise a new, more comprehensive chemical-weapons ban. Yet, many nations, including the United States, left the conference feeling that more needed to be done. Although the nations present supported a chemical-weapons ban, they failed to insist unanimously that sanctions be applied against violators.

Still, some headway was made toward a U.S.–Soviet chemical-weapons agreement. The treaty requirements formerly demanded by the Reagan Administration were somewhat eased by President George Bush when he advanced negotiations with the Soviets. He demonstrated that a U.S.–Soviet agreement could proceed and could perhaps even assist in facilitating a subsequent international chemical-weapons ban. Bush also determined that, while absolute verification may not be feasible, verification to permit detection of a "militarily significant quantity" of chemical weapons would be acceptable.

Fortunately, important recent scientific advances make verification a less troublesome issue. Alastair W. M. Hay of the University of Leeds, who has done extensive research on various methods to detect slight traces of chemicals, concluded that "verification can work and is practical as long as there is reasonable access." The new advances are largely due to the work of researchers at the University of Helsinki. The group isolated two hundred chemicals used in the production of supertoxins, which can now be accurately measured even in environments in which other chemicals are present.

Current detection methods are sufficiently accurate to pinpoint chemical plants that have been "sanitized" to avoid detection following the production of dangerous toxins. This can be accomplished through intrusive inspection procedures, which involve sampling the air and waste stream, taking wipe samples from equipment, and perhaps even dismantling pumps to examine the residue trapped within.

While it might still be possible to construct a facility

with the capacity to switch back and forth quickly between the production of legitimate chemical products and weapons agents, such a plant would be extremely costly and would need to be specifically designed for that purpose. Since there are few economically justifiable reasons to build a legitimate chemical plant with these unique change-over characteristics, such a facility would immediately raise the suspicions of the inspectors, who could then monitor it with a higher degree of precision.

Eventually, a global chemical-weapons treaty may result in the installation of tamper-proof sensors capable of recording the presence of suspicious chemicals over lengthy time intervals. In addition to the lab work completed on verification methods, a number of nations began experimenting with trial monitoring systems within their own countries, in the hope that one day a single internationally acceptable verification procedure may be devised.

Yet, even though detection systems have been vastly enhanced over the years, verification may still be problematic in other ways. One recurrent concern is that a country's chemical industry might be compromised by such procedures. Some of the chemicals commonly used in binary weapons, as well as those readily turned into supertoxins, also have peacetime industrial applications. If chemical concerns manufacturing pesticides and other nonmilitary products were subject to routine inspections, it might be difficult for them to insure that competitors did not become privy to valuable nonpatentable information pertinent to their product.

Researchers are presently working on measures to maintain the confidentiality of legitimate chemical companies. One method, called "sample now, analyze later," picks up bits of material on a moving tape at predetermined times without an inspector present at the site. When these samples are later analyzed, the researcher tests only for prohibited substances and therefore has no information on the legitimate uses of other substances present at the plant.

Another suggestion is that sensitive information on product production be retained in temper-proof bins or cabinets at the plant site. A number of private chemical companies in Japan, Britain, and the United States that favor an international chemical-weapons treaty are presently working on various inspection procedures to safeguard confidentiality.

Perhaps one of the most exciting developments in this area finally occurred in June 1990 when, after lengthy negotiations, an agreement was signed by both President Bush and President Mikhail Gorbachev that largely called for the destruction of the vast bulk of their respective nations' chemical-weapons stockpiles. According to a White House summary of the agreement, some of the major points of the accord are as follows:

❑ Destruction of at least 50 percent of declared stocks by the end of 1999.

❑ Reduction of declared stocks to five thousand agent tons by 2002.

❑ Cessation of chemical-weapons production by both countries upon entry into this agreement, without waiting for a global chemical-weapons ban.

❑ On-site inspections during and after the destruction process to confirm that destruction has taken place.

- Annual exchanges of data on the stockpile levels to facilitate monitoring of the declared stockpiles.

- Cooperation by both countries in developing and using safe, environmentally sound methods of destruction.

- Encouragement by the United States and the Soviet Union for all chemical-weapons-capable states to devise an acceptable international ban. Both countries took an initial step in that direction by exchanging data on declared chemical-weapons stockpiles.

Critics of the U.S.–Soviet agreement argue that the document is problematic, since adequate verification measures have not been finalized and because the Soviet Union currently lacks the equipment to safely dispose of its substantial chemical-weapons stockpile. Nevertheless, supporters of the pact believe this initiative will go a long way toward eliminating both Soviet and American arsenals of poison gas and will serve as an impetus to other nations to do the same. Although the agreement was not perfect, attaining an airtight program to abolish chemical weapons was unrealistic at that point. Many felt it was safer to live in a partially disarmed world than in one where both smaller nations and superpowers were actively engaged in creating sizable chemical-weapon arsenals. Perhaps an editorial in *The New York Times* best summarized the situation in stating, "Ronald Reagan was fond of the slogan 'trust but verify.' But Mr. Bush and Mr. Gorbachev know that in the face of a common danger, the creeping spread of chemical arms, it makes sense to trust even when they can't fully verify."

Yet, unfortunately, things did not go as well as planned. As the months passed, the U.S.–Soviet agreement experienced new difficulties. In June 1990, Presidents Bush and Gorbachev had signed only the treaty draft. The superpowers were supposed to sign the final document by the year's end. But that never happened, and now U.S. officials aren't sure if the Soviet Union is making a serious effort to follow through on its commitments.

One U.S. official described the situation this way: "There's been a hardening of positions across the spectrum of arms control negotiations in recent months. They are simply being more difficult to deal with. . . . We are having to go back and renegotiate things we thought we had already settled."

Part of the problem is that the Soviet Union still lacks an environmentally sound means by which to destroy its chemical-weapons stockpile. To worsen matters, there doesn't seem to be any urgency on the Soviets' part to rectify the situation. According to Richard Fieldhouse of the Natural Resources Defense Council, an environmental think tank in Washington, D.C., "There's a sense that the political momentum got a bit ahead of the technology, but more so for the Soviet Union than the United States. It's a matter of them deciding how hard they want to push the problem. Right now, they're fumbling and this problem is just going to get bigger as time goes on."

U.S. optimism about the treaty began to fade, as some Americans suspected that perhaps our government too readily trusted a longtime opponent. Their concerns deepened following the August 1991 failed coup to overthrow Soviet president Mikhail Gorbachev. There was some speculation that Gorbachev would now be free to improve relations with the West. Others felt, however, that the fate of U.S.–Soviet treaties was as uncertain as the future of the Soviet Union itself.

# 6

# DANGER! ENVIRONMENTAL AND MORAL RISKS

The eventual halt of chemical-weapons production and the reduction of stockpiles are worthwhile goals for the future. Yet, just as producing and maintaining these agents posed safety and environmental risks, their destruction entails some alarming hazards as well.

The army's challenge to implement safe, efficient disposal measures began even prior to the U.S.–Soviet pact, since Congress had already mandated a chemical-weapons destruction program to be completed by 1997. Its purpose was to destroy older, less stable stockpiles of chemical weapons, in order to create room for safer, more sophisticated forms. Estimated to cost over three billion dollars, the program was outlined in a document known as CD/711, prepared by the U.S. Army Aberdeen Proving Ground in Maryland. Among the stated goals in CD/711 was the hope that "in planning and implementing this disposal program, the United States would gain valuable experience and technical expertise which could prove helpful in our [international] negotiations."[1]

To initiate both CD/711 and our weapons-reduction agreement with the Soviets, the army had to decide where to destroy the weapons. Specialists needed to determine if it was more advantageous to dispose of U.S.-based chemical weapons at their stockpile sites or to transport them to a central location for the process. Following a lengthy government assessment, which supposedly considered both public opinion and environmental impact, it was decided that weapons would be destroyed at facilities in the following locations: Anniston, Alabama; Pine Bluff, Arkansas; Pueblo, Colorado; Newport, Indiana; Lexington, Kentucky; Aberdeen, Maryland; Umatilla, Oregon; Toole, Utah; and Johnson Atoll in the Pacific.

But the disposal program did not proceed unprotested, as environmentalists raised serious concerns about the fate of the surrounding human and animal populations, as well as about the actual physical landscape in the event of a mishap. They stressed that the army's past safety record in similar undertakings was less than ideal. The production, testing, and stockpiling of these agents had already caused some frightening episodes.

In one such instance, a low-flying military plane was less than one hundred miles from Salt Lake City when a valve on a tank of nerve gas on the carrier malfunctioned. The unanticipated release of the lethal gas killed nearly six thousand sheep grazing in the area. There was a loud public outcry, as critics pointed out that the poison gas could have fallen on a shopping district or near a school playground, rather than on livestock-grazing territory. A second air accident occurred when the pilot of a small plane was overcome by the accidental release of a tear gas canister on board. The plane crashed, killing the pilot and all four passengers.

There have been other disturbing incidents as well. Between 1952 and 1969, a minimum of 220 people at the army's Dugway Proving Ground in Utah (a chemical-weapons production site) were accidentally exposed to hazardous chemical agents. At least two of these individuals died.

Critics sometimes characterize portions of the Dugway facility as a "toxic wasteland." An assortment of unexploded chemical weapons, in addition to a deteriorating one-thousand-pound bomb (officials are unsure of its chemical content), lie untouched beneath the ground. A Dugway official described the situation: "The base will have to be off limits forever. A lot of stuff buried beneath the sand will not deteriorate or neutralize for many years."[2]

Concerned individuals stress that while all of Dugway's 175-mile expanse should ideally be fenced off, with prominent warning signs posted, only portions of the grounds are actually enclosed. Unfortunately, this fencing hasn't always kept intruders out. Dugway personnel admit that at times "tourists, students from nearby universities, and other personnel" have mistakenly wandered onto test-range areas.

Civilian workers have also been negatively affected by Dugway's toxic environment. In 1986, while nonmilitary contractors completed some construction there, several crew members accidentally hit a number of toxic-chemical canisters that had been haphazardly buried at the site years before. Those workers subsequently experienced painful headaches, nausea, exhaustion, and liver problems.

Such mishaps involving dangerous chemical agents make many individuals uneasy about the initiation of an extensive army disposal program at various sites throughout the nation. The safety issue in chemical-weapons disposal was again emphasized in April 1988, when Congress learned that the army discovered over one thousand leaking chemical weapons at numerous stockpile sites. A June 1988 in-house survey by the army's inspector general further noted that "chemical safety has slipped through a crack." The report added that the army "suffers from a lack of published policy guidelines, inadequate staffing, no systematic program of overview, and less than a clear statement of chemical safety responsibilities."

Still another report, issued by the U.S. Government Accounting Office in July 1988, faulted our chemical-warfare program for its inadequacy in considering such crucial environmental factors as the proximity of lab sites to both residential and business districts, as well as to surrounding natural landscape features. The report further indicated that there were "numerous deficiencies" in emergency contingency plans at production and storage sites.

Environmentalists fear that the army may not be prepared to dispose of large quantities of chemical agents and toxic substances. They vividly recall the negative environmental repercussions of former disposal projects. For instance, in 1960, toxic chemicals at a nerve-gas arsenal in Colorado's Rocky Mountains were poured through a large canal dug into the mountainous terrain. Within weeks, the region's first earthquake in over three quarters of a century shook the ground.

The site's substantial chemical-weapons disposal continued, but, after more than one hundred thousand gallons of the hazardous substances flowed into the earth and approximately fifteen hundred earthquake tremors occurred, the army stopped the program. Officials hoped to draw the toxic substances out of the ground, but this proved to be problematic. Engineers determined that, even if the toxic fluids were pumped out at the fastest possible rate, it would take over a thousand years to complete the process. Meanwhile, lethal substances may be slowly seeping into the water table.[3]

In response to criticism on a number of levels, the army attempted to improve its performance in both maintaining and disposing of chemical weapons. According to army spokesperson Major Richard Bridges, "We are doing everything in our power to make sure our installations and the communities surrounding them are afforded the safest possible practices, and we have no intention ever of injuring the public or our soldiers, our most precious commodity."[4]

To that end, the army drafted new safety regulations and filled key positions. But, although there has been some progress, the major admitted, "I cannot say with 100 percent certainty that every single environmental impact statement that is required for every installation that the army owns is complete, is current, and is on file."[5]

Despite the last-ditch efforts of environmentalists, disposal programs are currently under way in the United States. The United States also recently removed four hundred tons of chemical weapons from NATO storage dumps in Germany. This was a high-risk operation, since transporting one hundred thousand artillery shells loaded with sarin and VX nerve gas, by both truck and train through densely populated areas, involved considerable hazards.

To complete the task, the nerve-gas shells were first hoisted onto an eighty-truck convoy, which followed a route lined with nearly fifteen thousand German police officers. Additional backup forces included helicopters, riot police truck units, sharpshooters, and firefighters. The nerve gases were then placed on trains to Nordenham, Germany, and from there they were taken by ship to be destroyed at Johnson Island, a U.S. atoll in the Pacific. To minimize the risk of terrorists sabotaging the lethal cargo, the army did not disclose either the route or the sailing date of the ships carrying the artillery shells.

Although German citizens were relieved to be rid of the nerve-gas agents, plans for the weapons' incineration on Johnson Island, located about 825 miles southwest of Hawaii, set off protests throughout the Pacific. American Samoa, the Republic of the Marshall Islands, the Federated States of Micronesia, the Cook Islands, New Zealand, the governor of Hawaii, and environmental groups expressed concern as to whether the new 240-million-dollar incinerator on the island was adequately equipped to handle the massive disposal chore.

The safe disposal of chemical weapons is a complicated and painstaking procedure. First the weapons must be dismantled and the toxic substances separated from the explosive elements. Then the weapons' nerve-gas agents are chemically neutralized prior to incinerating all the weapon components at an extremely high temperature. If the incineration system is flawed in any way, the exhaust sent into the atmosphere may be extremely toxic.

Therefore, it was suggested that the Johnson Island incinerator operate for a year-and-a-half trial period before undertaking the nerve-gas disposal. Still another concern was that even "benign" incinerator smokestack emissions might contaminate the area's ocean food chain. However, the army defended its choice of Johnson Island on the grounds that there was no comparable facility within the continental United States. The army further stated that the incinerator's preliminary tests had proceeded without incident.

Despite their defeats, environmentalists, along with considerable numbers of involved citizens, continue to alert the general public to the dangers inherent in various chemical-weapons disposal programs. At times, weapon destruction in other countries has been disastrous. After Britain ceased its chemical-weapons production in the late 1950s, several haphazard attempts were made to bury or burn these stockpiled armaments at their storage sites. Today these areas remain too lethally toxic to enter.

The British also disposed of substantial quantities of mustard gas by loading the deadly cargo onto ships and sinking it in the sea. Unfortunately, now the floors of the Baltic Sea, the North Sea, and the Irish Sea are dotted with artillery shells that secrete lethal chemicals. At times, fishermen even accidentally catch these discarded munitions in their nets.

The chemical-weapons disposal problem in the Soviet Union is acute as well. This may be because the Soviets hope to dispose of their huge chemical-weapons stockpiles through the fairly new process of chemical neutralization rather than by incineration. But when the Soviets recently designed and built a chemical-weapons disposal plant near the Russian city of Chepayevsk, enraged local residents succeeded in blocking the facility's opening. In addition to environmental protests, there are also economic concerns over the high cost of chemical-weapons disposal at a time when the Soviet economy is weak. In describing the situation,

General V. K. Pikalov, former head of the Soviet Chemical Forces, said, "As you know, the economic situation in this country is very difficult now. I estimate that to destroy these fifty thousand metric tons of chemical weapons would cost at least twenty million dollars. But I can tell you that to destroy chemical weapons is much better than to make them. That is my opinion."[6]

Undoubtedly, there are serious obstacles to overcome in finding effective ways to dispose of chemical weapons. Yet if the Soviets eventually settle on a workable and financially feasible disposal option, and if the disposal process proceeds smoothly in the United States, the U.S.–Soviet dismantling agreement may eventually reduce concerns over chemical weapons.

Unfortunately, new developments in biological warfare suggest a potentially different scenario in that arena. As military interest in biological weapons peaked, skepticism among public-interest groups regarding some upcoming army endeavors increased. Environmentalists were intensely critical of the army's proposed 5.4-million-dollar biological-warfare research facility, slated for construction at Utah's Dugway Proving Ground, a longtime chemical-weapons center. While the army favored the site because of its sparse population, dry climate, and low winds, critics once again charged that preliminary safety and environmental checks had not been adequately established and tested.

Local residents and their elected officials, attending public hearings on the proposed facility, ardently expressed their opposition to the plant. Both Utah Governor Norman H. Bangerter and Senator Orrin G. Hatch supported their constituency in arguing that the military should find another site. Hatch described the army's plan as "reckless endangerment" and indicated that Johnson Island in the Pacific would be a more appropriate location for the lab, while Bangerter stressed that he remained "adamently opposed" to basing the facility in Utah.[7] A local television station and newspaper both ran editorials exposing the potential hazards inherent in the proposed plant's development and operation.

Concern over the plant was expressed by other factions as well. Arguing that the army's environmental-impact statement "doesn't deal at all with mass evacuation, mass quarantine, or emergency medical treatment," Jeremy Rifkin, president of the Foundation on Economic Trends, a Washington, D.C.–based public-interest group, stated that "this is a situation that's every bit as dangerous as a Three Mile Island or Chernobyl."[8] In 1985, opponents won a small victory in a lawsuit launched by the Foundation on Economic Trends against the Defense Department, and the lab's construction was temporarily postponed. The Defense Department agreed to a court settlement, requiring it to complete a twenty-one-month environmental-impact study of the possible ramifications of the Dugway lab's operation.

But biological-weapons opponents remain concerned about the eventual existence of the facility. They are especially skeptical of the Dugway lab, since it would be capable of producing new genetically engineered forms of bacteria and viruses, in addition to conventional biological-warfare agents such as anthrax, Q fever, tularemia, and others. The consequences of a possible mishap involving genetically designed organisms are especially frightening, since vaccines and cures cannot be developed for these strains. Concerned individuals fear lab workers might accidentally become infected with a new incurable disease if they cannot be vaccinated for it ahead of time.

Following the 1985 lawsuit to scuttle the proposed Dugway lab, the army characterized its biological-weapons defense program as well conceived and structured. In a recent environmental-impact report, the Defense Department states that it has implemented improved regulations that "assure adequate protection for the work force and virtually total protection for the external environment."

Nevertheless, critics of the biological-weapons program doubt both the accuracy and the truthfulness of the Defense Department's claims. As with chemical weapons, the army's history of safely testing biological agents is flawed. During the 1950s, the army secretly tested presumably harmless organisms that reacted like biological agents when released. The benign organisms were filtered into such densely populated places as New York City's subway system and the San Francisco Bay area. Over a decade and a half later, the army admitted that one of these widely tested "safe" organisms was later shown to be capable of killing both the aged and the infirm.[9]

The army also tested biological weapons in middle America during the 1950s and 1960s. In these instances, numerous biological agents were sprayed over largely unpopulated areas. To protect outlying towns, it was essential that army personnel remain informed of current wind trends so that lethal sprays would not be accidentally transported to populated areas. As an army testing report asserted, "Meteorological conditions were an absolute control factor in whether or not a test was permitted to start or continue."

Yet such precautions were not always heeded, as is indicated in an army summary recounting how the test results for one agent were not available because the wind scattered the organisms in every direction. The summary stated, "The agent can no longer be detected in four plots. . . . This, perhaps, was due in part to a heavy windstorm which cut into these plots and blew away the surface soil and organisms."

Supposedly, the army tests were to include measures to prevent the infectious organisms from ever reaching the Interstate 80 highway, located about thirty-five miles from the test site. Otherwise, researchers feared that passing motorists might be infected by anthrax spores and other disease organisms that were released into the air.

But there is evidence to indicate that anthrax spores eventually reached a portion of the highway. Once a cloud of these organisms floated just a mile above the road, while on another occasion a mist of anthrax spores blew over a small nearby town. Yet the army continued the testing program, thinking that as long as the exposure level remained low, there was no significant danger to the surrounding population.

But critics of the program questioned the army's ability to pinpoint accurate levels of these dangerous substances. Their lax measurement procedures were especially evident in an army report describing the test situations. It read, "No methods exist at this time to indicate reliably the concentration of anthrax spores reaching U.S. Highway 40 [now Interstate 80]. . . . Use of this [method of measuring biological agents] may lead to erroneous results, but at this time it represents the 'best guess' and, for that reason, the assumption is made."

In any case, measuring levels of released biological agents generally was not done to prevent hazardous public exposure, but rather to determine the potential effectiveness of the disease organisms. Researchers needed to be certain the germ agents would not be destroyed by natural elements if used against enemy forces in battle.

Although it is hoped that no one was harmed through these tests, it may be impossible to know if anyone traveling along Interstate 80 or living in an adjacent town was adversely affected. "The problem with all state epidemiological records is the quality and completeness of reporting from the community," said a doctor working on disease origins. "Most cases of mild to moderately severe respiratory illnesses are not going to be reported. Most influenza-type diseases (such as Q fever and others) are not reported."[10]

Similar concerns regarding biotechnology safety hazards were raised in other countries. In Japan, residents of Tokyo's heavily populated Shinjuku district protested a proposed biological-warfare lab. Opponents argued that an environmental-impact statement had not been prepared, and that even if strict safety standards were adhered to, it would still be nearly impossible to protect the local environment in the event of an accident. The protesters also expressed their disdain for the project's personnel, claiming that a number of the laboratory scientists were involved in Japan's biological-warfare experiments during World War II.

With the growing emphasis on biotechnology in the United States, biological-warfare opponents also questioned the government's defense program on a moral and ethical level. Yet, in accordance with the 1972 Biological and Toxin Weapons Convention Treaty, the army claimed that facilities such as the Dugway lab will not develop offensive weapons, but merely "test the effectiveness of equipment and procedures that have been developed for defense against attack with biological materials." Meanwhile, similar defense-funded research presently continues in both university and corporate settings in at least twenty-one states. The government never refers to these collective efforts as a biological-warfare program, but instead delicately labels the project "military biotechnology" or "biological-weapons defense work." They stress that such advanced research is essential to our nation's "preparedness" against an attack. One military researcher at the army's Institute for Infectious Diseases described their strategy when he said, "We'd be negligent if we weren't in a defensive posture."

But if this were true of even the proposed Dugway lab, then many of the facility's capabilities are unwarranted. Expressing his view of the lab and its potential, one scientist noted, "It's a joke really. There's no defense against these kinds of organisms [genetically altered weapons]. And if you can't defend against something, then why are we pouring money into it? There's something else going on that we don't know about."[11]

Defense program critics argue that the entire concept of a defense system to ward off the effects of a biological-weapons attack is unrealistic. To shield Americans under these circumstances, the entire population would have to be vaccinated well in advance of an enemy strike. Since we would have no way of knowing ahead of time which biological agents might be used, every man, woman, and child would need to be vaccinated against a multitude of infectious diseases.

To develop a more practical defense strategy, defense-funded scientists are presently working on drugs to repel groups of related biological weapons rather than a single contaminating agent. This is achieved through isolating their common means of attack and developing an effective vaccine. Another potential development involves creating a benign "transport" virus to send immune-inducing agents into the body to prevent a number of possible infections.

But other researchers argue that these approaches would be worthless in the long run. They stress that, even if scientists produced a vaccine to defend against many viruses, it is likely that the enemy would genetically alter the disease-producing organisms to render the vaccine useless. Sometimes this process occurs spontaneously. "Nature does this herself," one scientist explained. "A virus changes its clothes and comes back wearing a different coat. The military cannot make an indefinite number of vaccines to [defend against] an indefinite number of viruses."[12]

Some critics further argue that, in instances of biological warfare, the distinction between offensive and defensive research frequently becomes clouded. A biologist at the Massachusetts Institute of Technology asserted, "The notion of a biological-weapons defense research-and-development program is a fundamental misrepresentation. The title of such a program [biological-weapons defense or preparedness] implies that it is possible to defend one's civilian population from biological-warfare agents. In fact, the only real rationale for the development of a defense to a known agent is if one is planning to use that agent in an offensive mode."[13] Some scientists even feel it is impossible to ever conclusively separate offensive from defensive research in biological warfare, since at times it may be necessary to both design and manufacture destructive agents to develop vaccines against them.

Many researchers contend that biological-weapons programs are self-defeating in several ways. They fear the negative international consequences if continued work with biological weapons eventually draws the United States closer to using them. There is also the concern that such research tends to fuel a biological-weapons race, as nations feel compelled to compete with one another in this realm. The greater the proliferation of these weapons, the more likely it becomes that the dangerous organisms might one day fall into the hands of unscrupulous individuals.

Numerous scientists, appalled at the consequences of biological-weapons research, refuse to participate in such projects. They contend that any "success" in this field would only result in eventual widespread suffering and devastation. In one such instance, a civilian scientist turned down Defense Department funding to introduce penicillin-resistant germs into a bacteria responsible for pneumonia because the work "would have been a disservice to civilization."

A substantial group of socially conscious scientists throughout the country joined together to take a stand against continued biological-warfare research. The Committee for Responsible Genetics (CRG) and the Coalition for Universities in the Public Interest sponsored a nationwide pledge, in which researchers agreed never to "engage knowingly in research and teaching that will further the development of biological-warfare agents." According to the CRG, "The pledge campaign can help to reverse these trends that threaten to release a biological arms race. Our goal is to bring that pledge to every biological and biomedical researcher in the country."[14]

However, not all scientists feel negatively about research in this area. Some, working on biologically innovative projects, believe these advances may benefit both military and civilian populations. A number of researchers, who found it financially difficult to continue worthwhile research projects, foresee tangible accomplishments in the public health arena resulting from their present work. One scientist studying lassa fever, which accounts for about 30 percent of hospital deaths in Africa, stated, "It's difficult to get money to study diseases such as lassa fever. We've gone to major companies and been refused funds. One agency with a good [financial] track record is the army."[15]

While some scientists perceive dual benefits resulting from defense work, others undertake these projects to enhance the nation's military posture. They believe their highest moral obligation is to preserve and defend their country.

Some scientists who feel uncomfortable doing biological-warfare research may be torn between their personal disdain for the work and their desire to assist their country in times of crisis. That was the position of a number of scientists who developed biological agents during World War II because they believed that use of such weapons against the United States would leave the country militarily vulnerable. Yet, once the war ended, they refused to work on similar projects. "We were fighting a fire, and it seemed necessary to risk getting dirty as well as burnt,"[16] wrote one scientist of their efforts. Their stance sharply differed from that of other researchers, who felt that even a "righteous" war didn't justify inflicting pain and death on other human beings.

Interestingly, at times, scientists who have developed incapacitating rather than lethal chemical and biological weapons argue that they have actually reduced the widespread devastation commonly associated with combat. "If we do succeed in creating incapacitating systems which are able to substitute incapacitation for death, it appears to me that next to stopping war, this would be an important step forward,"[17] is how a scientist active in weapons research in the 1960s described his initial goals.

Still other scientists view the creation of truly devastating armaments as crucial in deterring war. They believe that if opposing nations are equally prepared to inflict massive suffering and destruction on one another, the likelihood that their weapons will ever be used is significantly decreased. As early as 1892, Albert Nobel advanced this argument to justify developing dynamite when he said, "On the day that two army corps can mutually annihilate each other in a second, all civilized nations will surely recoil with horror and disband their troops."[18]

Yet, researchers working on biological-warfare projects may still face troubling questions. Frequently their knowledge of new developments makes them uniquely aware of the potential dangers associated with their work. If these facts are not classified as government secrets, is a scientist morally obligated to alert the public to important issues of environmental and humanitarian concern? While some scientists feel they should use their prestige to influence public policy, others disagree. They believe scientists should not abuse their special access to information in order to influence social action, especially when some facets of the total picture may be beyond their area of expertise.

Depending on the scientist's particular specialty, there may be other moral considerations as well. Although their skills are often essential in biological-warfare programs, physicians may be especially ill at ease on these projects because of their profession's special role in preserving and extending life.

Many medical students in the United States still swear to the Hippocratic Oath, which states, "I will use treatment to help the sick according to my ability and judgment, but never with a view to injury and wrongdoing. Neither will I administer a poison to anybody even when asked to do so, nor will I suggest such a course." This view of medical morality was further reinforced by the World Medical Association's Code of Ethics, which says, "It is deemed unethical for doctors to weaken the physical and mental strength of a human being without therapeutic justification, and to employ scientific knowledge to imperil health or destroy life."

Therefore, doctors who are approached to work on germ-warfare research are frequently uncertain of the appropriate role for them in such undertakings. Some insist on working only on defensive measures, as was reflected in this quote from a physician who conducted germ-warfare research during World War II. He said, "There was much quiet, searching discussion among us regarding the place of doctors in such work.... A certain delicacy concentrated most of the physicians into principally or primarily defensive operations."[19] But, as the boundaries between offensive and defensive research become less sharply defined, the issue grows more complex. As a result, some doctors have gone a step further and emphatically refuse to involve themselves in any aspect of weapons research. In the final analysis, physicians, as well as other scientists, must decide individually whether greater harm or good will result from their participation.

Nevertheless, one highly respected molecular biologist recently reminded his colleagues that morality tends to be based on very subjective standards, which sometimes sway with both economic and political trends. He said, "Look how many good physicists, given the pressure of their times, were convinced to build [atomic] bombs. If we had to, we could build very frightening things very quickly."[20] Unfortunately, since biological weapons are now less expensive, easier to produce, and enhanced by genetic engineering, their accessibility may have already reduced present legal and moral restraints against their use in various parts of the world.

Some political analysts feel the best U.S. strategy would be to renounce biological weaponry rather than exhibit a renewed interest in it. They advocate active U.S. support of and leadership in achieving a more effective international ban on all forms of biological weaponry. These strategists believe that as long as the superpowers create and stockpile biological weapons, even if only for defensive purposes, countries who have threatened to use such weapons irresponsibly are also free to accumulate them. Even though the United States and other technologically advanced nations are not yet prepared to cast aside their stockpiles, analysts feel that strong international sanctions and penalties must be imposed on countries that abuse this horrific weaponry.

A former U.S. secretary of state may have best expressed this imperative when he stated, "At stake in all of this is not just the violation of codes of international conduct, but civilization itself. If we tolerate the breakdown of barriers against the use of chemical and biological weapons, such agents of mass destruction may come to be seen as both advantageous and legitimate in the pursuit of national security interests, as just another 'weapon of choice.' Countries that use [these] weapons in violation of international law are wrong, and they know it. We must not legitimize, by our acquiescence, a practice that will threaten all civilized societies."[21]

# ORGANIZATIONS CONCERNED WITH PEACE AND DISARMAMENT

**Arms Control Association**
11 Dupont Circle N.W., Suite 250
Washington, D.C. 20036
(202) 797-4626

**Center for Peace Studies (CPS)**
University of Akron
Akron, OH 44325-6201
(216) 375-7008

**Children as the Peacemakers (CATP)**
950 Battery Street, 2nd floor
San Francisco, CA 94111
(415) 981-0916

**Consortium On Peace, Research, Education, and Development (COPRED)**
4400 University Drive
George Mason University
Fairfax, VA 22030
(703) 323-2806

104 ❑ CHEMICAL AND BIOLOGICAL WARFARE

**Council for a Livable World (Disarmament)**
20 Park Plaza
Boston, MA 02116
(617) 542-2282

**Disarm Education Fund (Disarmament)**
36 E. 12th Street, 6th floor
New York, NY 10003
(212) 475-3232

**Foundation for Peace**
P.O. Box 244
Arlington, VA 22210
(703) 764-6465

**Generations for Peace**
1315 S.W. Park Avenue
Portland, OR 97201
(503) 222-2194

**Groundwork for a Just World**
11224 Kercheval
Detroit, MI 48214
(313) 822-2055

**Jane Addams Peace Association**
777 United Nations Plaza
New York, NY 10017
(212) 682-8830

**National Commission for Economic Conversion and Disarmament (NCECD)**
1621 Connecticut Avenue N.W., Suite 350
Washington, D.C. 20009
(202) 544-5059

**National Peace Institute Foundation**
110 Maryland Avenue N.E., Suite 409
Washington, D.C. 20002
(202) 546-9500

**National Research Council On Peace Strategy (NRCPS)**
241 W. 12th Street
New York, NY 10014
(212) 675-3839

**The Nerve Center (Disarmament)**
1917 E. 29th Street
Oakland, CA 94606
(415) 534-6904

**Non-Governmental Committee On Disarmament**
777 United Nations Plaza, Room 4A-2
New York, NY 10017
(212) 687-5340

**Peace Museum**
430 W. Erie Street
Chicago, IL 60610
(312) 440-1860

**Peace Studies Association**
Dept. of Sociology and Anthropology
Wright State University
Dayton, OH 45435
(513) 873-2942

**Promoting Enduring Peace**
P.O. Box 5103
Woodmont, CT 06460
(203) 878-4769

**U.S. Institute for Peace**
1550 M Street N.W., Suite 700
Washington, D.C. 20005
(202) 457-1700

**Veterans for Peace**
P.O. Box 3881
Portland, ME 04104
(267) 797-2770

**Vietnam Veterans Agent Orange Victims**
P.O. Box 2465
Darien, CT 06820-0465
(203) 323-7478

**Women for a Meaningful Summit (Disarmament)**
2401 Virginia Avenue N.W.
Washington, D.C. 20037
(202) 785-8497

**Women's International League for Peace and Freedom, U.S. Section (WILPF-US)**
1213 Roce Street
Philadelphia, PA 19107
(215) 563-7110

**Women's Strike for Peace (WSP)**
10216 Sutherland Road
Silver Spring, MD 20901
(301) 593-6948

**World Without War Council**
c/o Robert Pickus
1730 Martin Luther King, Jr., Way
Berkeley, CA 94709
(415) 845-1992

# END NOTES

**CHAPTER 1**

1. "Security Council Members Condemn Use of Chemical Weapons in Iran–Iraq Conflict," *UN Chronicle* 24 (August 1987): 34.
2. "Poisoned Winds of War," "Nova" (October 1990).
3. Russell Watson, "The Winds of Death, Eliminating Poison Gas Could Be Harder Than Controlling Nuclear Weapons," *Newsweek* 113 (January 16, 1989): 22.
4. "Poisoned Winds of War," *op. cit.*
5. Louise Lief, "Learning To Live with Import Controls; Will the Bonn Government Really Crack Down on German Businesses?" *U.S. News & World Report* 106 (January 23, 1989): 28.
6. Louise Lief and Steven Emerson, "The Uphill Fight To Contain Chemical Weapons," *U.S. News & World Report* 106 (January 9, 1989): 42.
7. Deborah Orin, "Chemical Plant Reported Ablaze in Libya," *New York Post*, 15 March 1990.
8. "Iraq Admits It Has Chemical Arms; Holds Deadly Threat over Israel," *The Star Ledger*, 3 April 1990.
9. "Poisoned Winds of War," *op. cit.*
10. *Ibid.*
11. Patrick E. Tyler, "U.S. Prepares for High Poison Gas Toll," *The New York Times*, 22 February 1991.
12. "If Iraq Uses Chemical Weapons," *U.S. News & World Report* 109 (August 20, 1990): 24.

13. "The New Merchants of Death," *World Press Review* 36 (March 1989): 13.
14. Russel Watson, *op. cit.*
15. Bill Turque, "The Spector of Iraq's Poison Gas," *Newsweek* 116 (August 20, 1990): 26.
16. Russell Watson, *op. cit.*

## CHAPTER 2

1. "Herbicide Linked to Cancer in Military Dogs," *The New York Times*, 20 June 1990.
2. John Grossman, "A War with Hope," *Health* 19 (June 1987): 86.
3. Keith Schneider, "American Legion to Sue U.S. Over Agent Orange," *The New York Times*, 2 August 1990.
4. House Government Operations Committee, "The Agent Orange Cover Up: A Case of Flawed Science and Political Manipulation," *House Report #101-672*, 9 August 1990, 18.
5. Marcia Barinaga, "Agent Orange: Congress Impatient for Answers," *Science* 245 (July 21, 1989): 249.
6. Janet Gardner, "New Agent Orange Research: Answers at Last?" *The Nation* 244 (April 11, 1987): 462.
7. *Ibid.*

## CHAPTER 3

1. U.S. Department of Defense Biological Defense Program, *Report to the Committee on Appropriations, House of Representatives*, May 1986, 3.
2. Melissa Hendricks, "Germ Wars," *Science News* 134 (December 17, 1988): 392.
3. *Ibid.*
4. Seth Shulman, "Poisons from the Pentagon," *The Progressive* 51 (November 1987): 17.
5. U.S. Department of Defense Biological Defense Program, *op. cit.*

## CHAPTER 4

1. Julian Perry Robinson, "The Changing Status of Chemical and Biological Warfare in World Armaments and Disarmament." SIPRI Yearbook (1982): 318.
2. "Prohibition of Chemical Weapons Conference Held in Paris," *Department of State Bulletin*, March 1989, 3.
3. Richard D. McCarthy, *The Ultimate Folly: War by Pestilence, Asphyxiation, and Defoliation* (New York: Knopf, 1969), p. 5.
4. Stockholm International Peace Research Institute (SIPRI), *The Problem of Chemical and Biological Warfare*, vol. 3: *CBW and the Law of War* (Stockholm: Almqvist & Wiksell, 1973), p. 151.
5. *Ibid.*
6. Barten J. Bernstein, "The Birth of the U.S. Biological Program," *Scientific American* 256 (June 1987): 16.
7. *Ibid.*
8. *Ibid.*
9. Charles Piller and Keith R. Yamamoto, *Gene Wars: Military Control Over the New Genetic Technologies* (New York: Beech Tree Books, 1988), p. 33.
10. Jeanne McDermott, *The Killing Winds: The Menace of Biological Warfare* (New York: Arbor House, 1987), p. 124.
11. Yuki Tanaka, "Poison Gas: The Story Japan Would Like To Forget," *Bulletin of the Atomic Scientist* 44 (October 1988): 14.

## CHAPTER 5

1. U.S. Department of Defense Biological Defense Program, *op. cit.*, p. 5.
2. Robert Bazell, "The Bees Did It," *New Republic* 2 (February 1987): 10.
3. Ashton et al., "Comparison of Yellow Rain and Bee Excrement" (paper presented at the annual meeting of the American Association for the Advancement of Science), Detroit, Michigan (May 31, 1983).

4. Rick Weiss, "Anthrax Outbreak: The Soviet Scenario," *Science News* 133 (May 23, 1988): 261.
5. *Ibid.*
6. *Ibid.*

**CHAPTER 6**

1. Max L. Friedersdorf, "Chemical Weapons Disposal Program," *Department of State Bulletin*, June 1989, 11.
2. Charles Piller and Keith R. Yamamoto, *op. cit.*, p. 52.
3. *Ibid.*, p. 53.
4. Melissa Hendricks, *op. cit.*, p. 394.
5. *Ibid.*
6. "Poisoned Winds of War," *op. cit.*
7. Rick Weiss, "Neighbors Bugged by Germ Warfare Lab," *Science News* 133 (April 9, 1988): 229.
8. "Biological Warfare Facility Debated," *Science News* 133 (February 13, 1988): 100.
9. Charles Piller, "Lethal Lies About Fatal Diseases," *The Nation* 247 (October 3, 1988): 272.
10. *Ibid.*, p. 274.
11. "Biological Warfare Facility Debated," p. 100.
12. Melissa Hendricks, *op. cit.*, p. 394.
13. Seth Shulman, *op. cit.*, p. 18.
14. *Ibid.*, p. 19.
15. Melissa Hendricks, *op. cit.*, p. 394.
16. Theodor Rosebury, "Medical Ethics and Biological Warfare," *Perspectives in Biology and Medicine* 6 (1962): 514.
17. Robert William Reid, *Tongues of Conscience: Weapons, Research, and the Scientist's Dilemma* (New York: Walker & Co., 1969), p. 315.
18. *Ibid.*
19. Theodor Rosebury, *op. cit.*
20. Russell Watson, *op. cit.*, p. 24.
21. "Prohibition of Chemical Weapons Conference Held in Paris," 5.

# FURTHER READINGS

## BOOKS

Bender, David L., ed. *The Arms Race: Opposing Viewpoints.* St. Paul, Minnesota: Greenhaven Press, 1982.

Dupuy, Ernest R. *The Encyclopedia of Military History; from 3500 B.C. to the Present.* 2nd rev. ed. New York: Harper and Row, 1986.

O'Neil, Richard, ed. *An Illustrated Guide to the Modern U.S. Army.* New York: Arco, 1984.

Paxman, Jeremy, and Robert Harris. *A Higher Form of Killing: The Secret Story of Gas and Germ Warfare.* New York: Hill and Wang, 1982.

Perrett, Bryan. *Desert Warfare: From Its Roman Origins to the Gulf Conflict.* New York: Sterling, 1989.

## ARTICLES

Beardsley, Tim, "Clearing the Air; Chemical Weapons Can Be Banned, Given the Political Will," *Scientific American* 260, March 1989, p. 17.

Beardsley, Tim, "Easier Said Than Done; Burning Chemical Weapons Is No Simple Process," *Scientific American* 263, September 1990, p. 48.

"Biological Weapons Proliferation," *Department of State Bulletin* 89, July 1989, p. 43.

"Conference on Disarmament Urged To Speed Work on Chemical Ban," *UN Chronicle* 27, June 1990, p. 30.

"A Deadly Solvent," *Time* 133, February 13, 1989, p. 41.

Dickson, David, "Fertile Ground for Arms Control," *Science* 243, February 24, 1989, p. 100.

Doerner, William R., "A Rush To Sign Up New Accords: After Years of Dickering Over Details, the Superpowers Suddenly Make Progress on Four Arms-Control Fronts," *Time*, 135 February 28, 1990, p. 19.

Evans, Harold, "A War of Nerves," *U.S. News & World Report* 106, January 16, 1989, p. 72.

Kestin, Hesh, "They May Not Be Weapons at All," *Forbes* 144, September 18, 1989, p. 45.

Lief, Louise, "Learning To Live with Export Controls: Will the Bonn Government Really Crack Down on German Business?" *U.S. News & World Report* 106, January 23, 1989, p. 28.

Marcuse, Elie, "An Equality of Terror: Missile & Chemical Warheads = WW III," *World Press Review* 36, March 1989, p. 17.

"The Poison This Time," *Time* 133, January 30, 1989, p. 45.

Salholz, Eloise, "Defense: A Chemical Reaction; Two U.S. Producers Tangle with the Pentagon," *Newsweek* 115, April 23, 1990, p. 26.

Schneider, Keith, "Legion Suing U.S. on Agent Orange; Veterans Charge Government Violated Law by Halting a Study on the Defoliant," *New York Times* 139, August 2, 1990, p. A11(N), col. 1.

Shulman, Seth, "Funding for Biological-Weapons Research Grows Amidst Controversy," *BioScience* 37, June 1987, p. 372.

Silbergeld, Ellen K., "Agent Orange Claims Should Be Paid Now," *The American Legion Magazine* 127, July 1989, p. 46.

"Small Fire, Much Smoke," *The Economist* 134, March 31, 1990, p. 42.

Smolowe, Jill, "Stumbling toward Armageddon? Iraq's Threats Against Israel Heat Up a Region That Keeps Growing More Dangerous, Even as the Superpowers Back Away from Unstinting Support for Their Respective Allies," *Time* 135, April 16, 1990, p. 30.

"Vietnam Veterans Sustain Cancer Threat," *Science News* 137, April 14, 1990, p. 236.

"Wages of War," *U.S. News & World Report* 109, September 10, 1990, p. 17.

# INDEX

Aberdeen Proving Ground, 17, 82
Abu Ibrahim, 24
Abu Nidal, 24
adamite (vomiting gas), 29
Afghanistan, 70
Agent Orange, 31–40, 55
American Chemical Society, 74–75
American Legion, 34–37
Amherst, Lord Jeffrey, 51
anthrax, 43, 48, 58, 72–73, 92
anti-crop weapons, 31
Army, U.S.:
   biological weapons and, 45–46, 49, 89–93
   chemical-weapons disposal by, 82–89
Australia group, 75–76

baking soda, 14, 54
ballistic missiles, long-range, 6
Bangerter, Norman H., 89–90
Barbouti, Ihsan, 8–9
Big Eye bomb, 75
binary weapons, 14, 69

Biological and Toxin Weapons Convention Treaty (1972), 49, 67–68, 93–94
   Soviet violations of, 70, 72–74
biological weapons, 26–28, 42–52, 54–56, 67–70, 72–74, 76, 89–101
   defined, 42
   early developments in, 51–52, 54–63
   environmental risks in disposal of, 89–93
   Japanese experiments with, 61–63
   moral and ethical risks of, 93–101
   types of, 42–48
   U.S. Army testing of, 91–93
biotechnology, 48, 49, 74, 93–94
birth defects, 32, 33, 35
bleach, 19
blister gas, 29
blood gases, 30
bone marrow, 1, 39
botulin, 44–45, 58
Bridges, Richard, 86

Burgasov, Petr, 73
Bush, George, 4, 23, 77, 79–81
Bush Administration, 34, 76

Caesar, Julius, 51
cancer, Agent Orange and, 32–34, 36, 39–40
Carter, Jimmy, 68
Carus, Seth, 26
CD/711, 82–83
Centers for Disease Control (CDC), 35–37, 39
Chemical Corps, U.S., 54
chemical defoliants, 31
chemicals, 75, 78–79
  suppliers of, 6–11, 13, 15
Chemical Warfare Review Commission, 48, 69
chemical weapons, 1–41, 67–72, 74–89
  Australia group and, 75–76
  binary, 14, 69
  biological weapons compared with, 49
  deaths from, 1, 3, 26, 39, 53, 54, 64
  defined, 28
  delivery of, 6, 27, 28, 76
  early developments in, 51–56, 60–61, 63–66
  German role in production of, 7–11
  in Iraq-Iran war, 1–4, 55, 75
  Iraq's use of, 1–5, 13–14, 16, 22, 23–24
  Libya's manufacturing of, 7–10
  manufacturing of, 5–10
  Persian Gulf war and, 14–23
  physical effects of, 1, 3, 4, 18–19, 28–40, 61, 64–65
  as poor man's weapons, 5–6, 25
  profits from, 9, 10
  protective measures against, 14–21, 25–26
  safety and environmental risks in disposal of, 82–89
  of Soviet Union, 68–71, 75–77, 79–81
  types of, 29–41
  United Nations investigation of use of, 2–4, 27
  verification and, 76–81
  in World War I, 25, 29, 30, 52–54
Chepayevsk, 88
chickens, 20
China, 55, 60–61, 62–63
chlorine, 29–30, 52
choking gas (phosgene), 30
Churchill, Winston, 59–60
Civil War, U.S., 52
Cloonan, Terry, 18
clothing, protective, 15, 17, 26, 54
Coalition for Universities in the Public Interest, 96
Committee for Responsible Genetics (CRG), 96–97
Conference on the Prohibition of Chemical Weapons, 76–77
Congress, U.S., 35, 50, 69, 74, 82

*see also* House of
  Representatives, U.S.
cyanogen chloride, 30

decontamination, 19
Defense Department, U.S., 36
  biological weapons and, 48,
  50, 69–70, 72–74, 90–91,
  94, 96
defoliants, chemical, 31
dengue, 44
designer weapons, 42–43,
  48–49
detection methods, 20, 77–78
dioxin, 32, 39–40
dogs, Agent Orange and, 32
"double chemical," 14
drugs, anti-chemical, 18–19,
  20, 23
Dugway Proving Ground, 84,
  89–91, 94

Edgewood Arsenal, 54
environmental risks:
  biological weapons and, 89–
  93
  chemical weapons and, 82–
  89
Environmental Support
  Group, 36
Ethiopia, 55

farmers, Kansas study of, 33,
  39, 40
Feuerwerger, Marvin, 22
Fieldhouse, Richard, 81
First International Peace
  Conference (1899), 52,
  53
Fitzwater, Marlin, 12

Ford, Gerald, 68
Fort Detrick, 57
Fort McClellan, 18
Foundation on Economic
  Trends, 9
Fox M93, 19–20
France, 4, 5, 53
French and Indian War, 51
FROG-7 missiles, 23

Galbraith, Peter, 4–5
gas masks, 14–15, 17, 18, 23,
  26, 54, 61
gas shelters, 25
genetic engineering, 48, 49,
  70, 74
Geneva Protocol (1925), 1–2,
  4, 6, 54–56, 67, 76
Germany, 5, 7–13, 15, 39–40
  as chemical supplier, 7–11,
  12, 13, 15
  U.S. removal of chemical
  weapons from, 86–87
  in World War I, 52–53
  in World War II, 31, 58–60
germ warfare, *see* biological
  weapons
Gorbachev, Mikhail, 79–81
Government Accounting
  Office, U.S., 85
Great Britain, 5, 9, 51, 55–56,
  79, 88
Greeks, ancient, 51
Gruinard, 43

Halabja, 2, 3
Hatch, Orrin G., 89–90
Hay, Alastair W. M., 77
Heisbourg, François, 25
Helsinki, University of, 77

118 ◻ INDEX

herbicides, 31, 55
  see also Agent Orange
Hippocratic Oath, 99
Hitler, Adolf, 59
Holocaust, 15, 31, 59
Hong Kong, 9
House of Representatives, U.S., 37, 39, 61–62, 70
Hussein, Saddam, 5, 13–14, 20–24, 27
  Persian Gulf war and, 14, 16, 20–23
Hydrochloric acid, 6–7
hydrogen cyanide, 3, 30

IBI (Ihsan Barbouti International), 8–9
Imhausen, Hippenstiel, 10
Imhausen–Chemie Company, 8–10
Iran, 4, 5, 75
  see also Iraq–Iran war
Iraq, 1–7, 9, 14, 15, 21, 27
  chemical weapons and, 1–5, 6–7, 13–14, 16, 21, 22, 23–24
  military deserters in, 23–24
  military power of, 5, 27
  in Persian Gulf war, 14–16, 20–23
Iraq–Iran war, 1–5, 55, 75
Ireland, 56
Israel, 12–16, 25
  Persian Gulf war and, 14–16, 22–23
Italy, 5, 39–40, 55

James, Frank, 61–62
Japan, 39–40, 79, 93
  in World War II, 55, 60–66, 93

Japan Steel Works, 11
Johnson Island, 87–88, 90

Kahn, Peter, 40
Khairallah, Adan, 2–3
Kurds, chemical weapons used against, 2–3, 4, 22, 55
Kuwait, Iraqi invasion of, 14–16, 21

lewisite, 30
Libya, 7–13, 75
lymphoma, 33, 34, 36, 39, 40

McNaugher, Thomas L., 18
Mahmoud, Sonia, 3
Microbiology and Virology Institute, 72
Middle East, see Persian Gulf war
*Military Biology and Biological Agents*, 31
missiles, 6, 22–23, 76
Mitterrand, François, 21
M20 Collective Protection Equipment, 17
Mukden, China, POW experiments in, 62–63
mustard gas (yperite), 2, 3, 6, 7, 26, 29, 53, 60–61

napalm, 23
National Academy of Science, 56
National Cancer Institute, 32, 33
nerve gas, 2, 7, 10, 14, 15, 26, 30–31
  disposal problems with, 83, 86–88

physical effects of, 18–19
  in World War II, 31, 58, 59
Netherlands, 7, 13
*New York Times*, 80
Nixon, Richard M., 67
Nobel, Albert, 98
nuclear weapons, 14, 25

Okunoshima Island, 63–66
Osirak nuclear reactor, 14

Pakistan, 7
Palestinians, 22
Pearson, Graham, 6
Pérez de Cuellar, Javier, 4
Persian Gulf war, 14–23
pesticide factories, 5, 7
Phillips Petroleum Company, 6
phosgene (choking gas), 30
phosphorus, white, 23
Physicians for Human Rights, 3
Pikalov, V. K., 89
plague, 46–47
poison gas, 6, 26, 29–31, 51, 52–54, 64–66
  bombs, 20–21, 28
  Iraq's use of, 2–4
  *see also* mustard gas; nerve gas
pollen, 70–72
porpheria, 39–40
Potawatomi Indians, 51
projectiles, chemical, 52, 53
pyridostignine tablets, 18

Qaddafi, Muammar, 7–8, 10–13, 24
Q fever, 43–44, 93

Rabata, chemical-weapons facility, 7–13
Reagan Administration, 34, 37, 69, 76, 77
Reagan, Ronald, 68–69, 76, 77
Reuterskin, Paul, 34
rice blast, 41
Rifkin, Jeremy, 90
Rocky Mountains, Colorado, 85
Romans, ancient, 51

Salman Pak, 27
Samarra, 7
sarin, 30, 86
Saudi Arabia, 5, 16–20
saxitoxin, 47
Schecter, Arnold, 40
Scotland, 9
SCUD missiles, 22–23
shock, chemical weapons and, 18
Society for Threatened Peoples, 10
Soviet Union:
  biological weapons of, 68–69, 72–74
  chemical weapons of, 68–71, 75–77, 79–81, 88–89
  U.S. and, 68–74, 76–77, 79–81, 89
State Department, U.S., 32
Stellman, Jeanne, 37–38
Stellman, Steven, 37–38
Stimson, Henry L., 57
Sverdlovsk, anthrax epidemic in, 72–73
Sweden, 25, 26, 39–40
Switzerland, 25
Syria, 25, 75

tabun, 30-31
Taibor, Shabtal, 15
tear gas, 29, 55
terrorism, 7, 24-25
thiodiglycol, 6
Third World, chemical weapons and, 5-6, 7-11, 25
tularemia, 44
2, 4-D, 33

United Nations, 2-4, 25, 27, 56
United States, 4, 52, 63, 67-101
   Agent Orange used by, *see* Agent Orange
   biological weapons research of, 45-46, 48-50, 56-58, 67, 69
   chemical weapons and, 20, 74-75, 82-89
   Geneva Protocol and, 55, 56, 67
   intelligence sources of, 6, 7, 8, 11-12, 13, 16, 21
   in Persian Gulf war, 16-21, 23
   Rabata fire and, 12-13
   Soviet Union and, 68-74, 76-77, 79-81, 89
   in World War II, 56-58

Venezuelan Equine Encephalitis (VEE), 46

verification, 76-81
Veterans Administration, U.S. (VA), 40
Veterans Affairs Department, U.S., 35
Vietnam Veterans of America, 36
Vietnam War, 31-41
   Agent Orange in, 31-40, 55
vomiting gas (adamite), 29
V-1 "buzz bombs," 59
VX, 30, 31, 75, 86

War Department, U.S., 57
War Research Service (WRS), 57
Webster, William, 27
wheat rust, 40-41
World Medical Association, Code of Ethics of, 99
World War I, 25, 29, 30, 52-54
World War II, 31, 55-66, 93, 97-98

yellow fever, 47-48
yellow rain, 70-72
yperite, *see* mustard gas
Ypres, attacks on, 52-53

ZDF, 13
Zumwalt, Elmo, III, 38-39
Zumwalt, Elmo R., Jr., 38-39